the daughter of time

the daughter of time

Josephine Tey

Truth Is the daughter of time
Old Proverb

A BERKLEY MEDALLION BOOK
published by
BERKLEY PUBLISHING CORPORATION

BERKLEY MEDALLION EDITION, AUGUST, 1959
8th Printing, December, 1970 (New Edition)
TENTH PRINTING

SBN 425-01927-6

BERKLEY MEDALLION BOOKS are published by
Berkley Publishing Corporation
200 Madison Avenue
New York, N.Y. 10016

BERKLEY MEDALLION BOOKS ® TM 757,375

Printed in the United States of America

CHAPTER ONE

Grant lay on his high white cot and stared at the ceiling. Stared at it with loathing. He knew by heart every last minute crack on its nice clean surface. He had made maps of the ceiling and gone exploring on them; rivers, islands, and continents. He had made guessing games of it and discovered hidden objects; faces, birds, and fishes. He had made mathematical calculations of it and rediscovered his childhood; theorems, angles, and triangles. There was practically nothing else he could do but look at it. He hated the sight of it.

He had suggested to The Midget that she might turn his bed around a little so that he could have a new patch of ceiling to explore. But it seemed that that would spoil the symmetry of the room, and in hospitals symmetry ranked just a short head behind cleanliness and a whole length in front of Godliness. Anything out of the parallel was hospital profanity. Why didn't he read? she asked. Why didn't he go on reading some of those expensive brand-new novels that his friends kept on bringing him?

"There are far too many people born into the world, and far too many words written. Millions and millions of them pouring from the presses every minute. It's a horrible thought."

"You sound constipated," said The Midget.

The Midget was Nurse Ingham, and she was in sober fact a very nice five-feet-two, with everything in just proportion. Grant called her The Midget to compensate himself for being bossed around by a piece of Dresden china which he could pick up in one hand. When he was on his feet, that is to say. It was not only that she told him what he might or might not do, but she dealt with his six-feet-odd with an off-hand ease that Grant found humiliating. Weights meant nothing, apparently, to The Midget. She tossed mattresses around with the absent-minded grace of a plate spinner. When she was off duty he was attended to by The Amazon, a goddess with arms like the limb of a beech tree. The Amazon was Nurse Darroll, who came from Gloucestershire and was homesick each daffodil season. (The Midget came from Lytham St. Anne's, and there was no daffodil nonsense about her.) She had large soft hands and large soft cow's eyes and she always looked very sorry for you, but the slightest physical exertion set her breathing like a suction-pump. On the whole Grant found it even more humiliating to be treated as a dead weight than to be treated as if he were no weight at all.

Grant was bed-borne, and a charge on The Midget and The Amazon, because he had fallen through a trap-door. This, of course, was the absolute in humiliation; compared with which the heavings of The Amazon and the light slingings of The Midget were a mere corollary. To fall through a trap-door was the ultimate in absurdity; pantomimic, bathetic, grotesque. At the moment of his disappearance from the normal level of perambulation he had been in hot pursuit of Benny Skoll, and the fact that Benny had careened round the next corner slap into the arms of Sergeant Williams provided the one small crumb of comfort in an intolerable situation.

Benny was now "away" for three years, which was very satisfactory for the lieges, but Benny would get time off for good behaviour. In hospitals there was no time off for good behaviour.

Grant stopped staring at the ceiling, and slid his eyes sideways at the pile of books on his bedside table; the gay expensive pile that The Midget had been urging on his attention. The top one, with the pretty picture of Valetta in unlikely pink, was Lavinia Fitch's annual account of a blameless heroine's tribulations. In view of the representation of the Grand Harbour on the cover, the present Valerie or Angela or Cecile or Denise must be a naval wife. He had opened the book only to read the kind message that Lavinia had written inside.

The Sweat and the Furrow was Silas Weekley being

6

earthly and spade-conscious all over seven hundred pages. The situation, to judge from the first paragraph, had not materially changed since Silas's last book: mother lying-in with her eleventh upstairs, father laid-out after his ninth downstairs, eldest son lying to the Government in the cow-shed, eldest daughter lying with her lover in the hay-loft, everyone else lying low in the barn. The rain dripped from the thatch, and the manure steamed in the midden. Silas never omitted the manure. It was not Silas's fault that its steam provided the only uprising element in the picture. If Silas could have discovered a brand of steam that steamed downwards, Silas would have introduced it.

Under the harsh shadows and highlights of Silas's jacket was an elegant affair of Edwardian curlicues and Baroque nonsense, entitled *Bells on Her Toes.* Which was Rupert Rouge being arch about vice. Rupert Rouge always seduced you into laughter for the first three pages. About Page Three you noticed that Rupert had learned from that very arch (but of course not vicious) creature George Bernard Shaw that the easiest way to sound witty was to use that cheap and convenient method, the paradox. After that you could see the jokes coming three sentences away.

The thing with a red gun-flash across a night-green cover was Oscar Oakley's latest. Toughs talking out of the corners of their mouths in synthetic American that had neither the wit nor the pungency of the real thing. Blondes, chromium bars, breakneck chases. Very remarkably bunk.

The Case of the Missing Tin-Opener, by John James Mark, had three errors of procedure in the first two pages, and had at least provided Grant with a pleasant five minutes while he composed an imaginary letter to its author.

He could not remember what the thin blue book at the bottom of the pile was. Something earnest and statistical, he thought. Tsetse flies, or calories, or sex behaviour, or something.

Even in that, you knew what to expect on the next page. Did no one, any more, no one in all this wide world, change their record now and then? Was everyone nowa-days thirled to a formula? Authors today wrote so much to a pattern that their public expected it. The public talked

7

about "a new Silas Weekley" or "a new Lavinia Fitch" exactly as they talked about "a new brick" or "a new hairbrush." They never said "a new book by" whoever it might be. Their interest was not in the book but in its newness. They knew quite well what the book would be like.

It might be a good thing, Grant thought as he turned his nauseated gaze away from the motley pile, if all the presses of the world were stopped for a generation. There ought to be a literary moratorium. Some Superman ought to invent a ray that would stop them all simultaneously. Then people wouldn't send you a lot of fool nonsense when you were flat on your back, and bossy bits of Meissen wouldn't expect you to read them.

He heard the door open, but did not stir himself to look. He had turned his face to the wall, literally and metaphorically.

He heard someone come across to his bed, and closed his eyes against possible conversation. He wanted neither Gloucestershire sympathy nor Lancashire briskness just now. In the succeeding pause a faint enticement, a nostalgic breath of all the fields of Grasse, teased his nostrils and swam about his brain. He savoured it and considered. The Midget smelt of lavender dusting powder, and The Amazon of soap and iodoform. What was floating expensively about his nostrils was *L'Enclos Numéro Cinq*. Only one person of his acquaintance used L'Enclos Number Five. Marta Hallard.

He opened an eye and squinted up at her. She had evidently bent over to see if he was asleep, and was now standing in an irresolute way—if anything Marta did could be said to be irresolute—with her attention on the heap of all too obviously virgin publications on the table. In one arm she was carrying two new books, and in the other a great sheaf of white lilac. He wondered whether she had chosen white lilac because it was her idea of the proper floral offering for winter (it adorned her dressing-room at the theatre from December to March) or whether she had taken it because it would not detract from her black-and-white chic. She was wearing a new hat and her usual pearls; the pearls which he had once been the means of recovering for her. She looked very handsome, very Pari-

8

sian, and blessedly unhospital-like.

"Did I waken you, Alan?"

"No. I wasn't asleep."

"I seem to be bringing the proverbial coals," she said, dropping the two books alongside their despised brethren. "I hope you will find these more interesting than you seem to have found that lot. Didn't you even try a little teensy taste of our Lavinia?"

"I can't read anything."

"Are you in pain?"

"Agony. But it's neither my leg nor my back."

"What then?"

"It's what my cousin Laura calls 'the prickles of boredom.' "

"Poor Alan. And how right your Laura is." She picked a bunch of narcissi out of a glass that was much too large for them, dropped them with one of her best gestures into the wash-basin, and proceeded to substitute the lilac. "One would expect boredom to be a great yawning emotion, but it isn't, of course. It's a small niggling thing."

"Small nothing. It's like being beaten with nettles."

"Why don't you take up something?"

"Improve the shining hour?"

"Improve your mind. To say nothing of your soul and your temper. You might study one of the philosophies. Yoga, or something like that. But I suppose an analytical mind is not the best kind to bring to the consideration of the abstract."

"I did think of going back to algebra. I have an idea that I never did algebra justice, at school. But I've done so much geometry on that damned ceiling that I'm a little off mathematics."

"Well, I suppose it is no use suggesting jig-saws to someone in your position. How about cross-words. I could get you a book of them, if you like."

"God forbid."

"You could invent them, of course. I have heard that that is more fun than solving them."

"Perhaps. But a dictionary weighs several pounds. Besides, I always did hate looking up something in a reference book."

"Do you play chess? I don't remember. How about

9

chess problems? White to play and mate in three moves, or something like that."

"My only interest in chess is pictorial."

"Pictorial?"

"Very decorative things, knights and pawns and what-not. Very elegant."

"Charming. I *could* bring you along a set to play with. All right, no chess. You could do some academic investigating. That's a sort of mathematics. Finding a solution to an unsolved problem."

"Crime, you mean? I know all the case-histories by heart. And there is nothing more that can be done about any of them. Certainly not by someone who is flat on his back."

"I didn't mean something out of the files at the Yard. I meant something more—what's the word?—something classic. Something that has puzzled the world for ages."

"As what, for instance?"

"Say, the casket letters."

"Oh, *not* Mary Queen of Scots!"

"Why not?" asked Marta, who like all actresses saw Mary Stuart through a haze of white veils.

"I could be interested in a bad woman but never in a silly one."

"*Silly?*" said Marta in her best lower-register Electra voice.

"*Very* silly."

"Oh, Alan, how can you!"

"If she had worn another kind of headdress no one would ever have bothered about her. It's that cap that seduces people."

"You think she would have loved less greatly in a sun-bonnet?"

"She never loved greatly at all, in any kind of bonnet."

Marta looked as scandalised as a lifetime in the theatre and an hour of careful make-up allowed her to.

"Why do you think that?"

"Mary Stuart was six feet tall. Nearly all out-size women are sexually cold. Ask any doctor."

And as he said it he wondered why, in all the years since Marta had first adopted him as a spare escort when she needed one, it had not occurred to him to wonder

10

whether her notorious level-headedness about men had something to do with her inches. But Marta had not drawn any parallels; her mind was still on her favourite queen.

"At least she was a martyr. You'll have to allow her that."

"Martyr to what?"

"Her religion."

"The only thing she was a martyr to was rheumatism. She married Darnley without the Pope's dispensation, and Bothwell by Protestant rites."

"In a moment you'll be telling me she wasn't a prisoner!"

"The trouble with you is that you think of her in a little room at the top of a castle, with bars on the windows and a faithful old attendant to share her prayers with her. In actual fact she had a personal household of sixty persons. She complained bitterly when it was reduced to a beggarly thirty, and nearly died of chagrin when it was reduced to two male secretaries, several women, an embroiderer, and a cook or two. And Elizabeth had to pay for all that out of her own purse. For twenty years she paid, and for twenty years Mary Stuart hawked the crown of Scotland round Europe to anyone who would start a revolution and put her back on the throne that she had lost; or, alternatively, on the one Elizabeth was sitting on."

He looked at Marta and found that she was smiling.

"Are they a little better now?" she asked.

"Are what better?"

"The prickles."

He laughed.

"Yes. For a whole minute I had forgotten about them. That is at least one good thing to put down to Mary Stuart's account!"

"How do you know so much about Mary?"

"I did an essay about her in my last year at school."

"And didn't like her, I take it."

"Didn't like what I found out about her."

"You don't think her tragic, then."

"Oh, yes, very. But not tragic in any of the ways that popular belief makes her tragic. Her tragedy was that she was born a queen with the outlook of a suburban housewife. Scoring off Mrs. Tudor in the next street is

11

harmless and amusing; it may lead you into unwarrantable indulgence in hire-purchase, but it affects only yourself. When you use the same technique on kingdoms the result is disastrous. If you are willing to put a country of ten million people in pawn in order to score off a royal rival, then you end by being a friendless failure." He lay thinking about it for a little. "She would have been a wild success as a mistress at a girl's school."

"Beast!"

"I meant it nicely. The staff would have liked her, and all the little girls would have adored her. That is what I meant about her being tragic."

"Ah, well. No casket letters, it seems. What else is there? The Man in the Iron Mask."

"I can't remember who that was, but I couldn't be interested in anyone who was being coy behind some tinplate. I couldn't be interested in anyone at all unless I could see his face."

"Ah, yes. I forgot your passion for faces. The Borgias had wonderful faces. I should think they would provide a little mystery or two for you to dabble in if you looked them up. Or there was Perkin Warbeck, of course. Imposture is always fascinating. Was he or wasn't he? A lovely game. The balance can never come down wholly on one side or the other. You push it over and up it comes again, like one of those weighted toys."

The door opened and Mrs. Tinker's homely face appeared in the aperture surmounted by her still more homely and historic hat. Mrs. Tinker had worn the same hat since first she began to "do" for Grant, and he could not imagine her in any other. That she did possess another one he knew, because it went with something that she referred to as "me blue." Her "blue" was an occasional affair, in both senses, and never appeared at 19 Tenby Court. It was worn with a ritualistic awareness, and having been worn it was used in the event as a yardstick by which to judge the proceedings. ("Did you enjoy it, Tink? What was it like?" "Not worth putting on me blue for.") She had worn it to Princess Elizabeth's wedding, and to various other royal functions, and had indeed figured in it for two flashing seconds in a newsreel shot of the Duchess of Kent cutting a ribbon, but to Grant it was a mere

12

report; a criterion of the social worth of an occasion. A thing was or was not worth putting on "me blue" for.

"I 'eard you 'ad a visitor," said Mrs. Tinker, "and I was all set to go away again when I thought the voice sounded familiar like, and I says to meself: 'It's only Miss Hallard,' I says, so I come in."

She was carrying various paper bags and a small tight bunch of anemones. She greeted Marta as woman to woman, having been in her time a dresser and having therefore no exaggerated reverence for the goddesses of the theatre world, and looked askance at the beautiful arrangement of lilac sprays that had blossomed under Marta's ministrations. Marta did not see the glance but she saw the little bunch of anemones and took over the situation as if it were something already rehearsed.

"I squander my vagabond's hire on white lilac for you, and then Mrs. Tinker puts my nose out of joint by bringing you the Lilies of the Field."

"Lilies?" said Mrs. Tinker, doubtfully.

"Those are the Solomon in all his glory things. The ones that toiled not, neither did they spin."

Mrs. Tinker went to church only for weddings and christenings, but she belonged to a generation that had been sent to Sunday school. She looked with a new interest at the little handful of glory incased by her woollen glove.

"Well, now. I never knew that. Makes more sense that way, don't it? I always pictured them arums. Fields and fields of arums. Awful expensive, you know, but a bit depressing. So they was coloured? Well, why can't they say so? What do they have to call them lilies for!"

And they went on to talk about translation, and how misleading Holy Writ could be ("I always wondered what bread on the waters was," Mrs. Tinker said) and the awkward moment was over.

While they were still busy with the Bible, The Midget came in with extra flower vases. Grant noticed that the vases were designed to hold white lilac and not anemones. They were tribute to Marta; a passport to further communing. But Marta never bothered about women unless she had an immediate use for them; her tact with Mrs. Tinker had been mere *savior faire;* a conditioned reflex. So

13

The Midget was reduced to being functional instead of social. She collected the discarded narcissi from the washbasin and meekly put them back into a vase. The Midget being meek was the most beautiful sight that had gladdened Grant's eyes for a long time.

"Well," Marta said, having finished her arrangement of the lilac and placed the result where he could see it, "I shall leave Mrs. Tinker to feed you all the titbits out of those paper bags. It couldn't be, could it, Mrs. Tinker darling, that one of those bags contains any of your wonderful bachelor's buttons?"

Mrs. Tinker glowed.

"You'd like one or two maybe? Fresh outa me oven?"

"Well, of course I shall have to do penance for it afterwards—those little rich cakes are death on the waist—but just give me a couple to put in my bag for my tea at the theatre."

She chose two with a flattering deliberation ("I like them a little brown at the edges"), dropped them into her handbag, and said: "Well, au revoir, Alan. I shall look in, in a day or two, and start you on a sock. There is nothing so soothing, I understand, as knitting. Isn't that so, nurse?"

"Oh, yes, indeed. A lot of my gentlemen patients take to knitting. They find it whiles away the time very nicely."

Marta blew him a kiss from the door and was gone, followed by the respectful Midget.

"I'd be surprised if that hussy is any better than she ought to be," Mrs. Tinker said, beginning to open the paper bags. She was not referring to Marta.

CHAPTER TWO

But when Marta came back two days later it was not with knitting needles and wool. She breezed in, very dashing in a Cossack hat worn at a casual rake that must have taken her several minutes at her mirror, just after lunch.

"I haven't come to stay, my dear. I'm on my way to the theatre. It's matinée day, God help me. Tea trays and morons. And we've all got to the frightful stage when the lines have ceased to have any meaning at all for us. I don't think this play is ever coming off. It's going to be like those New York ones that run by the decade instead of by the year. It's too frightening. One's mind just won't stay on the thing. Geoffrey dried up in the middle of the second act last night. His eyes nearly popped out of his head. I thought for a moment he was having a stroke. He said afterwards that he had no recollection of anything that happened between his entrance and the point where he came to and found himself half-way through the act."

"A black-out, you mean?"

"No. Oh, no. Just being an automaton. Saying the lines and doing the business and thinking of something else all the time."

"If all reports are true that's no unusual matter where actors are concerned."

"Oh, in moderation, no. Johnny Garson can tell you how much paper there is in the house while he is sobbing his heart out on someone's lap. But that's different from being 'away' for half an act. Do you realise that Geoffrey had turned his son out of the house, quarrelled with his mistress, and accused his wife of having an affaire with his best friend all without being aware of it?"

"What *was* he aware of?"

"He says he had decided to lease his Park Lane flat to Dolly Dacre and buy that Charles the Second house at Richmond that the Latimers are giving up because he has got that Governor's appointment. He had thought about the lack of bathrooms and decided that the little upstairs room with the eighteenth-century Chinese paper would make a very good one. They could remove the beautiful paper and use it to decorate that dull little room downstairs at the back. It's full of Victorian paneling, the dull little room. He had also reviewed the drainage, wondered if he had enough money to take the old tiling off and replace it, and speculated as to what kind of cooking range they had in the kitchen. He had just decided to get rid of the shrubbery at the gate when he found himself face to face with me, on a stage, in the presence of nine hundred and eighty-seven people, in the middle of a speech. Do you wonder that his eyes popped? I see that you have managed to read at least one of the books I brought you—if the rumpled jacket is any criterion."

"Yes. The mountain one. It was a godsend. I lay for hours looking at the pictures. Nothing puts things in perspective as quickly as a mountain."

"The stars are better, I find."

"Oh, *no*. The stars merely reduce one to the status of an amoeba. The stars take the last vestige of human pride, the last spark of confidence, from one. But a snow mountain is a nice human-size yardstick. I lay and looked at Everest and thanked God that I wasn't climbing those slopes. A hospital bed was a haven of warmth and rest and security by comparison, and The Midget and The Amazon two of the highest achievements of civilisation."

"Ah, well, here are some more pictures for you."

Marta up-ended the quarto envelope she was carrying, and spilled a collection of paper sheets over his chest.

"What is this?"

"Faces," said Marta, delightedly. "Dozens of faces for you. Men, women, and children. All sorts, conditions, and sizes."

He picked a sheet off his chest and looked at it. It was an engraving of a fifteenth-century portrait. A woman.

"Who is this?"

16

"Lucrezia Borgia. Isn't she a duck?"

"Perhaps, but are you suggesting that there was any mystery about her?"

"Oh, yes. No one has ever decided whether she was her brother's tool or his accomplice."

He discarded Lucrezia, and picked up a second sheet. This proved to be the portrait of a small boy in late-eighteenth-century clothes, and under it in faint capitals was printed the words: Louis XVII.

"Now there's a *beautiful* mystery for you," Marta said. "The Dauphin. Did he escape or did he die in captivity?"

"Where did you get all these?"

"I routed James out of his cubby-hole at the Victoria and Albert, and made him take me to a print shop. I knew he would know about that sort of thing, and I'm sure he has nothing to interest him at the V. and A."

It was so like Marta to take it for granted that a Civil Servant, because he happened also to be a playwright and an authority on portraits, should be willing to leave his work and delve about in print shops for her pleasure.

He turned up the photographs of an Elizabethan portrait. A man in velvet and pearls. He turned the back to see who this might be and found that it was the Earl of Leicester.

"So that is Elizabeth's Robin," he said. "I don't think I ever saw a portrait of him before."

Marta looked down on the virile fleshy face and said: "It occurs to me for the first time that one of the major tragedies of history is that the best painters didn't paint you till you were past your best. Robin must have been quite a man. They say Henry the Eighth was dazzling as a young man, but what is he now? Something on a playing card. Nowadays we *know* what Tennyson was like before he grew that frightful beard. I must fly. I'm late as it is. I've been lunching at the Blague, and so many people came up to talk that I couldn't get away as early as I meant to."

"I hope your host was impressed," Grant said, with a glance at the hat.

"Oh, yes. She knows about hats. She took one look and said 'Jacques Tous, I take it.' "

"She!" said Grant surprised.

17

"Yes. Madeleine March. And it was I who was giving her luncheon. Don't look so astonished: it isn't tactful. I'm hoping, if you must know, that she'll write me that play about Lady Blessington. But there was such a to-ing and fro-ing that I had no chance to make any impression on her. However, I gave her a wonderful meal. Which reminds me that Tony Bittmaker was entertaining a party of seven. Magnums galore. How do you imagine he keeps going?"

"Lack of evidence," Grant said, and she laughed and went away.

In the silence he went back to considering Elizabeth's Robin. What mystery was there about Robin?

Oh, yes. Amy Robsart, of course.

Well, he wasn't interested in Amy Robsart. He didn't care how she had fallen down stairs, or why.

But he spent a very happy afternoon with the rest of the faces. Long before he had entered the Force he had taken a delight in faces, and in his years at the Yard that interest had proved both a private entertainment and a professional advantage. He had once in his early days dropped in with his Superintendent at an identification parade. It was not his case, and they were both there on other business, but they lingered in the background and watched while a man and a woman, separately, walked down the line of twelve nondescript men, looking for the one they hoped to recognise.

"Which is Chummy, do you know?" the Super had whispered to him.

"I don't know," Grant had said, "but I can guess."

"You can? Which do you make it?"

"The third from the left."

"What is the charge?"

"I don't know. Don't know anything about it."

His chief had cast him an amused glance. But when both the man and the woman had failed to identify anyone and had gone away, and the line broke into a chattering group, hitching collars and settling ties preparatory to going back to the street and the world of everyday from which they had been summoned to assist the Law, the one who did not move was the third man from the left. The third man from the left waited submissively for his escort and was led to his cell again.

"Strewth!" the Superintendent had said. "One chance out of twelve, and you made it. That was good going. He picked your man out of the bunch," he said in explanation to the local Inspector.

"Did you know him?" the Inspector said, a little surprised. "He's never been in trouble before, as far as we know."

"No, I never saw him before. I don't even know what the charge is."

"Then what made you pick him?"

Grant had hesitated, analysing for the first time his process of selection. It had not been a matter of reasoning. He had not said: "That man's face has this characteristic or that characteristic, therefore he is the accused person." His choice had been almost instinctive; the reason was in his subconscious. At last, having delved into his subconscious, he blurted: "He was the only one of the twelve with no lines on his face."

They had laughed at that. But Grant, once he had pulled the thing into the light, saw how his instinct had worked and recognised the reasoning behind it. "It sounds silly, but it isn't," he said. "The only adult entirely without face lines is the idiot."

"Freeman's no idiot, take it from me," the Inspector broke in. "A very wide-awake boy he is, believe me."

"I didn't mean that. I mean that the idiot is irresponsible. The idiot is the standard of irresponsibility. All those twelve men in that parade were thirty-ish, but only one had an irresponsible face. So I picked him at once."

After that it had become a mild joke at the Yard that Grant could "pick them at sight." And the Assistant Commissioner had once said teasingly: "Don't tell me that you believe that there is such a thing as a criminal face, Inspector."

But Grant had said no, he wasn't as simple as that. "If there was only one kind of crime, sir, it might be possible; but crimes being as wide as human nature, if a policeman started to put faces into categories he would be sunk. You can tell what the normal run of over-sexed women look like by a walk down Bond Street any day between five and six, and yet the most notorious nymphomaniac in London looks like a cold saint."

"Not so saintly of late; she's drinking too much these days," the A.C. had said, identifying the lady without difficulty; and the conversation had gone on to other things.

But Grant's interest in faces had remained and enlarged until it became a conscious study. A matter of case records and comparisons. It was, as he had said, not possible to put faces into any kind of category, but it was possible to characterise individual faces. In a reprint of a famous trial, for instance, where photographs of the principal actors in the case were displayed for the public's interest, there was never any doubt as to which was the accused and which the judge. Occasionally, one of the counsel might on looks have changed places with the prisoner in the dock—counsel were after all a mere cross-section of humanity, as liable to passion and greed as the rest of the world, but a judge had a special quality; an integrity and a detachment. So, even without a wig, one did not confuse him with the man in the dock, who had had neither integrity nor detachment.

Marta's James, having been dragged from his "cubbyhole," had evidently enjoyed himself, and a fine selection of offenders, or their victims, kept Grant entertained until The Midget brought his tea. As he tidied the sheets together to put them away in his locker his hand came in contact with one that had slipped off his chest and had lain all the afternoon unnoticed on the counterpane. He picked it up and looked at it.

It was the portrait of a man. A man dressed in the velvet cap and slashed doublet of the late fifteenth century. A man about thirty-five or thirty-six years old, lean and clean shaven. He wore a rich jewelled collar, and was in the act of putting a ring on the little finger of his right hand. But he was not looking at the ring. He was looking off into space.

Of all the portraits Grant had seen this afternoon this was the most individual. It was as if the artist had striven to put on canvas something that his talent was not sufficient to translate into paint. The expression in the eyes—

that most arresting and individual expression—had defeated him. So had the mouth: he had not known how to make lips so thin and so wide look mobile, so the mouth was wooden and a failure. What he had best succeeded in was the bone structure of the face: the strong cheekbones, the hollows below them, the chin too large for strength.

Grant paused in the act of turning the thing over, to consider the face a moment longer. A judge? A soldier? A prince? Someone used to great responsibility, and responsible in his authority. Someone too conscientious. A worrier; perhaps a perfectionist. A man at ease in a large design, but anxious over details. A candidate for gastric ulcer. Someone, too, who had suffered ill-health as a child. He had that incommunicable, that indescribable look that childhood suffering leaves behind it, less positive than the look on a cripple's face, but as inescapable. This the artist had both understood and translated into terms of paint. The slight fullness of the lower eyelid, like a child that has slept too heavily; the texture of the skin; the old-man look in a young face.

He turned the portrait over to look for a caption.

On the back was printed: *Richard the Third. From the portrait in the National Portrait Gallery. Artist Unknown.*

Richard the Third.

So that was who it was. Richard the Third. Crouchback. The monster of nursery stories. The destroyer of innocence. A synonym for villainy.

He turned the paper over and looked again. Was that what the artist had tried to convey when he had painted those eyes? Had what he had seen in those eyes been the look of a man haunted?

He lay a long time looking at that face; at those extraordinary eyes. They were long eyes, set close under the brows; the brows slightly drawn in that worried, over-conscientious frown. At first glance they appeared to be peering; but as one looked one found that they were in fact withdrawn, almost absent-minded.

When The Midget came back for his tray he was still staring at the portrait. Nothing like this had come his way for years. It made La Giaconda look like a poster.

The Midget examined his virgin teacup, put a practised

hand against the teapot's tepid cheek, and pouted. She had better things to do, she conveyed, than bring him trays for him to ignore.

He pushed the portrait at her.

What did she think of it? If that man were her patient what would be her verdict?

"Liver," she said crisply, and bore away the tray in heel-tapping protest, all starch and blond curls.

But the surgeon, strolling in against her draught, kindly and casual, had other views. He looked at the portrait, as invited, and said after a moment's interested scrutiny:

"Poliomyelitis."

"Infantile paralysis?" Grant said; and remembered all of a sudden that Richard III had a withered arm.

"Who is it?" the surgeon asked.

"Richard the Third."

"Really? That's interesting."

"Did you know that he had a withered arm?"

"Had he? I didn't remember that. I thought he was a hunchback."

"So he was."

"What I do remember is that he was born with a full set of teeth and ate live frogs. Well, my diagnosis seems to be abnormally accurate."

"Uncanny. What made you choose polio?"

"I don't quite know, now that you ask me to be definitive. Just the look of the face, I suppose. It's the look one sees on the face of a cripple child. If he was born hunchbacked that probably accounts for it and not polio. I notice the artist has left out the hump."

"Yes. Court painters have to have a modicum of tact. It wasn't until Cromwell that sitters asked for 'warts and all.' "

"If you ask me," the surgeon said, absent-mindedly considering the splint on Grant's leg. "Cromwell started that inverted snobbery from which we are all suffering to-day. 'I'm a plain man, I am; no nonsense about me.' And no manners, grace, or generosity, either." He pinched Grant's toe with detached interest. "It's a raging disease. A horrible perversion. In some parts of the States, I understand, it's as much as a man's political life is worth to go to some constituencies with his tie tied and his coat on.

That's being stuffed-shirt. The beau ideal is to be one of the boys. That's looking very healthy," he added, referring to Grant's big toe, and came back of his own accord to the portrait lying on the counterpane.

"Interesting," he said, "that about the polio. Perhaps it really was polio, and that accounts for the shrunken arm." He went on considering it, making no movement to go. "Interesting, anyhow. Portrait of a murderer. Does he run to type, would you say?"

"There isn't a murder type. People murder for too many different reasons. But I can't remember any murderer, either in my own experience, or in case-histories, who resembled him."

"Of course he was *hors concours* in his class, wasn't he? He couldn't have known the meaning of scruple."

"No."

"I once saw Olivier play him. The most dazzling exhibition of sheer evil, it was. Always on the verge of toppling over into the grotesque, and never doing it."

"When I showed you the portrait," Grant said, "before you knew who it was, did you think of villainy?"

"No," said the surgeon, "no, I thought of illness."

"It's odd, isn't it? I didn't think of villainy either. And now that I know who it is, now that I've read the name on the back, I can't think of it as anything but villainous."

"I suppose villainy, like beauty, is in the eye of the beholder. Well, I'll look in again towards the end of the week. No pain to speak of now?"

And he went away, kindly and casual as he had come.

It was only after he had given the portrait further puzzled consideration (it piqued him to have mistaken one of the most notorious murderers of all time for a judge; to have transferred a subject from the dock to the bench was a shocking piece of ineptitude) that it occurred to Grant that the portrait had been provided as the illustration to a piece of detection.

What mystery was there about Richard III?

And then he remembered. Richard had murdered his two boy nephews, but no one knew how. They had merely disappeared. They had disappeared, if he remembered rightly, while Richard was away from London. Richard had sent someone to do the deed. But the mystery of the children's actual fate had never been solved. Two skeletons had turned up—under some stairs?—in Charles II's day, and had been buried. It was taken for granted that the skeletons were the remains of the young princes, but nothing had ever been proved.

It was shocking how little history remained with one after a good education. All he knew about Richard III was that he was the younger brother of Edward IV. That Edward was a blond six-footer with remarkable good looks and a still more remarkable way with women; and that Richard was a hunchback who usurped the throne on his brother's death in place of the boy heir, and arranged the death of that heir and his small brother to save himself any further trouble. He also knew that Richard had died at the battle of Bosworth yelling for a horse, and that he was the last of his line. The last Plantagenet.

Every schoolboy turned over the final page of Richard III with relief, because now at last the Wars of the Roses were over and they could get on to the Tudors, who were dull but easy to follow.

When The Midget came to tidy him up for the night, Grant said: "You don't happen to have a history book, by any chance, do you?"

"A history book? No. What would I be doing with a history book." It was not a question, so Grant did not try to provide an answer. His silence seemed to fret her.

"If you really want a history book," she said presently, "you could ask Nurse Darroll when she brings your supper. She has all her school books on a shelf in her room and it's quite possible she has a history among them."

How like The Amazon to keep her school books! he thought. She was still homesick for school as she was homesick for Gloucestershire everytime the daffodils bloomed. When she lumbered into the room, bearing his cheese pudding and stewed rhubarb, he looked at her with a tolerance that bordered on the benevolent. She ceased to be a large female who breathed like a suction-pump and became a potential dispenser of delight.

Oh yes, she had a history book, she said. Indeed, she rather thought that she had two. She had kept all her school books because she had loved school.

It was on the tip of Grant's tongue to ask her if she had

kept her dolls, but he stopped himself in time.

"And of course I loved history," she said. "It was my favourite subject. Richard the Lionheart was my hero."

"An intolerable bounder," Grant said.

"Oh, no!" she said, looking wounded.

"A hyperthyroid type," Grant said pitilessly. "Rocketing to and fro about the earth like a badly made firework. Are you going off duty now?"

"Whenever I've finished my trays."

"Could you find that book for me tonight?"

"You're supposed to be going to sleep, not staying awake over history books."

"I might as well read some history as look at the ceiling—which is the alternative. Will you get it for me?"

"I don't think I could go all the way up to the Nurses' Block and back again tonight for someone who is rude about the Lionheart."

"All right," he said. "I'm not the stuff that martyrs are made of. As far as I'm concerned Coeur-de-Lion is the pattern of chivalry, the chevalier sans peur et sans reproche, a faultless commander and a triple D.S.O. Now will you get the book?"

"It seems to me you've sore need to read a little history," she said, smoothing a mitred sheet-corner with a large admiring hand, "so I'll bring you the book when I come past. I'm going out to the pictures anyhow."

It was nearly an hour before she reappeared, immense in a camel-hair coat. The room lights had been put out and she materialised into the light of his reading-lamp like some kindly genie.

"I was hoping you'd be asleep," she said. "I don't really think you should start on these tonight."

"If there is anything that is likely to put me to sleep," he said, "it would be an English history book. So you can hold hands with a clear conscience."

"I'm going with Nurse Burrows."

"You can still hold hands."

"I've no patience with you," she said patiently and faded backwards into the gloom.

She had brought two books.

One was the kind of history book known as a Historical Reader. It bore the same relation to history as Stories

25

from the Bible bears to Holy Writ. Canute rebuked his courtiers on the shore, Alfred burned the cakes, Raleigh spread his cloak for Elizabeth, Nelson took leave of Hardy in his cabin on the *Victory*, all in nice clear large print and one-sentence paragraphs. To each episode went one full-page illustration.

There was something curiously touching in the fact that The Amazon should treasure this childish literature. He turned to the fly-leaf to see if her name was there. On the fly-leaf was written:

Ella Darroll,
   Form III
      Newbridge High School
         Newbridge,
            Gloucestershire.
               England
                  Europe,
                     The World
                        The Universe.

This was surrounded by a fine selection of coloured transfers.

Did all children do that, he wondered? Write their names like that, and spend their time in class making transfers? He certainly had. And the sight of those squares of bright primitive colour brought back his childhood as nothing had for many years. He had forgotten the excitement of transfers. That wonderfully satisfying moment when you began the peeling-off and saw that it was coming perfectly. The adult world held few such gratifications. A clean smacking drive at golf, perhaps, was the nearest. Or the moment when your line tightened and you knew that the fish had struck.

The little book pleased him so much that he went through it at his leisure. Solemnly reading each childish story. This, after all, was the history that every adult remembered. This was what remained in their minds when tonnage and poundage, and ship money, and Laud's Liturgy, and the Rye House Plot, and the Triennial Acts, and all the long muddle of schism and shindy, treaty and treason, had faded from their consciousness.

The Richard III story, when he came to it, was called

The Princes in the Tower, and it seemed that young Ella had found the Princes a poor substitute for Coeur-de-Lion, since she had filled every small O throughout the tale with neat pencil shading. The two golden-haired boys who played together in the sunbeam from the barred window in the accompanying picture had each been provided with a pair of anachronistic spectacles, and on the blank back of the picture-page someone had been playing Noughts and Crosses. As far as young Ella was concerned the Princes were a dead loss.

And yet it was a sufficiently arresting little story. Macabre enough to delight any child's heart. The innocent children; the wicked uncle. The classic ingredients in a tale of classic simplicity.

It had also a moral. It was the perfect cautionary tale.

But the King won no profit from his wicked deed. The people of England were shocked by his cold-blooded cruelty and decided that they would no longer have him for King. They sent for a distant cousin of Richard's, Henry Tudor, who was living in France, to come and be crowned King in his stead. Richard died bravely in the battle which resulted, but he had made his name hated throughout the country and many deserted him to fight for his rival.

Well, it was neat but not gaudy. Reporting at its simplest.

He turned to the second book.

The second book was the School History proper. The two thousand years of England's story were neatly parcelled into compartments for ready reference. The compartments, as usual, were reigns. It was no wonder that one pinned a personality to a reign, forgetful that that personality had known and lived under other kings. One put them in pigeon-holes automatically. Pepys: Charles II. Shakespeare: Elizabeth. Marlborough: Queen Anne. It never crossed one's mind that someone who had seen Queen Elizabeth could also have seen George I. One had been conditioned to the reign idea from childhood.

However it did simplify things when you were just a

27

policeman with a game leg and a concussed spine hunting up some information on dead and gone royalties to keep yourself from going crazy.

He was surprised to find the reign of Richard III so short. To have made oneself one of the best-known rulers in all those two thousand years of England's history, and to have had only two years to do it in, surely augured a towering personality. If Richard had not made friends he had certainly influenced people.

The history book, too, thought that he had personality.

Richard was a man of great ability, but quite unscrupulous as to his means. He boldly claimed the crown on the absurd grounds that his brother's marriage with Elizabeth Woodville had been illegal and the children of it illegitimate. He was accepted by the people, who dreaded a minority, and began his reign by making a progress though the south, where he was well received. During this progress, however, the two young Princes who were living in the Tower, disappeared, and were believed to have been murdered. A serious rebellion followed, which Richard put down with great ferocity. In order to recover some of his lost popularity he held a Parliament, which passed useful statutes against Benevolences, Maintenance, and Livery.

But a second rebellion followed. This took the form of an invasion, with French troops, by the head of the Lancaster branch, Henry Tudor. He encountered Richard at Bosworth, near Leicester, where the treachery of the Stanleys gave the day to Henry. Richard was killed in battle, fighting courageously, leaving behind him a name hardly less infamous than that of John.

What on earth were Benevolences, Maintenance, and Livery?

And how did the English like having the succession decided for them by French troops?

But, of course, in the days of the Roses, France was still a sort of semi-detached part of England; a country much less foreign to an Englishman than Ireland was. A fifteenth-century Englishman went to France as a matter of course; but to Ireland only under protest.

He lay and thought about that England. The England over which the Wars of the Roses had been fought. A green, green England; with not a chimney-stack from Cumberland to Cornwall. An England still unhedged, with great forests alive with game, and wide marshes thick with wild-fowl. An England with the same small group of dwellings repeated every few miles in endless permutation: castle, church, and cottages; monastery, church, and cottages; manor, church, and cottages. The strips of cultivation round the cluster of dwellings, and beyond that the greenness. The unbroken greenness. The deep-rutted lanes that ran from group to group, mired to bog in the winter and white with dust in the summer; decorated with wild roses or red with hawthorn as the seasons came and went.

For thirty years, over this green uncrowded land, the Wars of the Roses had been fought. But it had been more of a blood feud than a war. A Montague and Capulet affair; of no great concern to the average Englishman. No one pushed in at your door to demand whether you were York or Lancaster and to hale you off to a concentration camp if your answer proved to be the wrong one for the occasion. It was a small concentrated war; almost a private party. They fought a battle in your lower meadow, and turned your kitchen into a dressing-station, and then moved off somewhere or other to fight a battle somewhere else, and a few weeks later you would hear what had happened at that battle, and you would have a family row about the result because your wife was probably Lancaster and you were perhaps York, and it was all rather like following rival football teams. No one persecuted you for being a Lancastrian or a Yorkist, any more than you would be persecuted for being an Arsenal fan or a Chelsea follower.

He was still thinking of that green England when he fell asleep.

And he was not a whit wiser about the two young Princes and their fate.

CHAPTER THREE

"Can't you find something more cheerful to look at than that thing?" The Midget asked next morning, referring to the Richard portrait which Grant had propped up against the pile of books on his bed-side table.

"You don't find it an interesting face?"

"Interesting! It gives me the willies. A proper Dismal Desmond."

"According to the history books he was a man of great ability."

"So was Bluebeard."

"And considerable popularity, it would seem."

"So was Bluebeard."

"A very fine soldier, too," Grant said wickedly, and waited. "No Bluebeard offers?"

"What do you want to look at that face for? Who was he anyway?"

"Richard the Third."

"Oh, well, I ask you!"

"You mean that's what you expected him to look like."

"Exactly."

"Why?"

"A murdering brute, wasn't he?"

"You seem to know your history."

"Everyone knows that. Did away with his two little nephews, poor brats. Had them smothered."

"Smothered?" said Grant, interested. "I didn't know that."

"Smothered with pillows." She banged his own pillows with a fragile vigorous fist, and replaced them with speed and precision.

"Why smothering? Why not poison?" Grant inquired.

"Don't ask me. I didn't arrange it."

"Who said they were smothered?"

"My history book at school said it."

"Yes, but whom was the history book quoting?"

"Quoting? It wasn't quoting anything. It was just giving facts."

"Who smothered them, did it say?"

"A man called Tyrrel. Didn't you do any history, at school?"

"I attended history lessons. It is not the same thing. Who was Tyrrel?"

"I haven't the remotest. A friend of Richard's."

"How did anyone know it was Tyrrel?"

"He confessed."

"*Confessed?*"

"After he had been found guilty, of course. Before he was hanged."

"You mean that this Tyrrel was actually hanged for the murder of the two Princes?"

"Yes, of course. Shall I take that dreary face away and put up something gayer? There were quite a lot of nice faces in that bundle Miss Hallard brought you yesterday."

"I'm not interested in nice faces. I'm interested only in dreary ones; in 'murdering brutes' who are 'men of great ability.' "

"Well, there's no accounting for tastes," said The Midget inevitably. "And *I* don't have to look at it, thank goodness. But in my humble estimation it's enough to prevent bones knitting, so help me it is."

"Well, if my fracture doesn't mend you can put it down to Richard III's account. Another little item on that account won't be noticed, it seems to me."

He must ask Marta when next she looked in if she too knew about this Tyrrel. Her general knowledge was not very great, but she had been educated very expensively at a highly approved school and perhaps some of it had stuck.

But the first visitor to penetrate from the outside world proved to be Sergeant Williams; large and pink and scrubbed-looking; and for a little Grant forgot about battles long ago and considered wide boys alive today.

31

Williams sat planted on the small hard visitors' chair, his knees apart and his pale blue eyes blinking like a contented cat's in the light from the window, and Grant regarded him with affection. It was pleasant to talk shop again; to use that elliptical, allusive speech that one uses only with another of one's trade. It was pleasant to hear the professional gossip, to talk professional politics; to learn who was on the mat and who was on the skids.

"The Super sent his regards," Williams said as he got up to go, "and said if there was anything he could do for you to let him know." His eyes, no longer dazzled by the light, went to the photograph propped against the books. He leant his head sideways at it, "Who's the bloke?"

Grant was just about to tell him when it occurred to him that here was a fellow policeman. A man as used, professionally, to faces as he was himself. Someone to whom faces were of daily importance.

"Portrait of a man by an unknown fifteenth-century painter," he said. "What do you make of it?"

"I don't know the first thing about painting."

"I didn't mean that. I meant what do you make of the subject?"

"Oh. Oh, I see." Williams bent forward and drew his bland brows into a travesty of concentration. "How do you mean: make of it?"

"Well, where would you place him? In the dock or on the bench?"

Williams considered for a moment, and then said with confidence: "Oh, on the bench."

"You would?"

"Certainly. Why? Wouldn't you?"

"Yes. But the odd thing is that we're both wrong. He belongs in the dock."

"You surprise me," Williams said, peering again. "Do you know who he was, then?"

"Yes. Richard the Third."

Williams whistled.

"So that's who it is, is it! Well, well. The Princes in the Tower, and all that. The original Wicked Uncle. I suppose, once you know, you can see it, but off-hand it wouldn't occur to you. I mean, that he was a crook. He's the spit of old Halsbury, come to think of it, and if

32

Halsbury had a fault at all it was that he was too soft with the bastards in the dock. He used to lean over backwards to give them the benefit in his summing-up."

"Do you know how the Princes were murdered?"

"I don't know a thing about Richard III except that his mother was two years conceiving him."

"What! Where did you get that tale?"

"In my school history, I suppose."

"You must have gone to a very remarkable school. Conception was not mentioned in any history book of mine. That is what made Shakespeare and the Bible so refreshing as lessons; the facts of life were always turning up. Did you ever hear of a man called Tyrrel?"

"Yes; he was a con. man on the P. & O. boats. Drowned in the *Egypt*."

"No; I mean, in history."

"I tell you, I never knew any history except 1066 and 1603."

"What happened in 1603?" Grant asked, his mind still on Tyrrel.

"We had the Scots tied to our tails for good."

"Better than having them at our throats every five minutes. Tyrrel is said to be the man who put the boys out of the way."

"The nephews? No, it doesn't ring a bell. Well, I must be getting along. Anything I can do for you?"

"Did you say you were going to Charing Cross Road?"

"To the Phoenix, yes."

"You could do something for me."

"What is that?"

"Go into one of the bookshops and buy me a History of England. An adult one. And a Life of Richard III, if you can find one."

"Sure, I'll do that."

As he was going out he encountered The Amazon, and looked startled to find anything as large as himself in nurse's uniform. He murmured a good-morning in an abashed way, cast a questioning glance at Grant, and faded into the corridor.

The Amazon said that she was supposed to be giving Number Four her blanket bath but that she had to look in to see if he was convinced.

33

"Convinced?"

About the nobility of Richard Cœur-de-Lion.

"I haven't got round to Richard the First yet. But keep Number Four waiting a few moments longer and tell me what you know about Richard III."

"Ah, those poor lambs!" she said, her great cow's eyes soft with pity.

"Who?"

"Those two precious little boys. It used to be my nightmare when I was a kiddie. That someone would come and put a pillow over my face when I was asleep."

"Is that how it was done: the murder?"

"Oh, yes. Didn't you know? Sir James Tyrrel rode back to London when the court was at Warwick, and told Dighton and Forrest to kill them, and then they buried them at the foot of some stairs under a great mound of stones."

"But it doesn't say that in the book you lent me."

"Oh, that book is just history-for-exams, if you know what I mean. You don't get really interesting history in swot books like that."

"And where did you get the juicy gossip about Tyrrel, may one ask?"

"It isn't gossip," she said, hurt. "You'll find it in Sir Thomas More's history of his time. And you can't find a more respected or trustworthy person in the whole of history than Sir Thomas More, now can you?"

"No. It would be bad manners to contradict Sir Thomas."

"Well, that's what Sir Thomas says, and, after all, he was alive then and knew all those people to talk to."

"Dighton and Forrest?"

"No, of course not. But Richard, and the poor Queen, and those."

"The Queen? Richard's Queen?"

"Yes."

"Why 'poor'?"

"He led her an awful life. They say he poisoned her. He wanted to marry his niece."

"Why?"

"Because she was the heir to the throne."

34

"I see. He got rid of the two boys, and then wanted to marry their eldest sister."

"Yes. He couldn't marry either of the boys, you see."

"No, I suppose even Richard the Third never thought of that one."

"So he wanted to marry Elizabeth so as to feel safer on the throne. Actually, of course, she married his successor. She was Queen Elizabeth's grandmother. It always used to please me that Elizabeth was a little bit Plantagenet. I never was very fond of the Tudor side. Now I must go, or Matron will be here on her round before I have Number Four tidied up."

"That would be the end of the world."

"It would be the end of *me*," she said, and went away.

Grant took the book she had left him off the pile again, and tried to make head or tail of the Wars of the Roses. He failed. Armies marched and counter-marched. York and Lancaster succeeded each other as victors in a bewildering repetition. It was as meaningless as watching a crowd of dodgem cars bumping and whirling at a fair.

But it seemed to him that the whole trouble was implicit, the germ of it sown, nearly a hundred years earlier, when the direct line was broken by the deposition of Richard II. He knew all about that because he had in his youth seen *Richard of Bordeaux* at the New Theatre; four times he had seen it. For three generations the usurping Lancasters had ruled England: Richard of Bordeaux's Henry unhappily but with fair efficiency, Shakespeare's Prince Hal with Agincourt for glory and the stake for zeal, and his son in half-witted muddle and failure. It was no wonder if men hankered after the legitimate line again, as they watched poor Henry VI's inept friends frittering away the victories in France while Henry nursed his new foundation of Eton and besought the ladies at court to cover up their bosoms.

All three Lancasters had had an unlovely fanaticism which contrasted sharply with the liberalism of the Court which had died with Richard II. Richard's live-and-let-live methods had given place, almost overnight, to the burning of heretics. For three generations heretics had burned. It was no wonder if a less public fire of discontent had begun to smoulder in the heart of the man in the street.

Especially since there, before their eyes, was the Duke of York. Able, sensible, influential, gifted, a great prince in his own right, and by blood the heir of Richard II. They might not desire that York should take the place of poor silly Henry, but they did wish that he would take over the running of the country and clean up the mess.

York tried it, and died in battle for his pains, and his family spent much time in exile or sanctuary as a result.

But when the tumult and the shouting was all over, there on the throne of England was the son who had fought alongside him in that struggle, and the country settled back happily under that tall, flaxen, wenching, exceedingly beautiful but most remarkably shrewd young man, Edward IV.

And that was as near as Grant would ever come to understanding the Wars of the Roses.

He looked up from his book to find Matron standing in the middle of the room.

"I did knock," she said, "but you were lost in your book."

She stood there, slender and remote; as elegant in her way as Marta was; her white-cuffed hands clasped loosely in front of her narrow waist; her white veil spreading itself in imperishable dignity; her only ornament the small silver badge of her diploma. Grant wondered if there was anywhere in this world a more unshakable poise than that achieved by the matron of a great hospital.

"I've taken to history," he said. "Rather late in the day."

"An admirable choice," she said. "It puts things in perspective." Her eye lighted on the portrait and she said: "Are you York or Lancaster?"

"So you recognize the portrait."

"Oh, yes. When I was a probationer I used to spend a lot of time in the National. I had very little money and very sore feet, and it was warm in the Gallery and quiet and it had plenty of seats." She smiled a very little, looking back from her present consequence to that young, tired, earnest creature she had been. "I liked the Portrait Gallery best because it gave one the same sense of proportion that reading history does. All those Importances who had made such a to-do over so much in their day. All just

36

names. Just canvas and paint. I saw a lot of that portrait in those days." Her attention went back to the picture. "A most unhappy creature," she said.

"My surgeon thinks it is poliomyelitis."

"Polio?" She considered it. "Perhaps. I hadn't thought of it before. But to me it has always seemed to be intense unhappiness. It is the most desperately unhappy face that I have ever encountered—and I have encountered a great many."

"You think it was painted later than the murder, then?"

"Oh, yes. Obviously. He is not a type that would do anything lightly. A man of that calibre. He must have been well aware of how—heinous the crime was."

"You think he belonged to the type who can't live with themselves any more."

"What a good description! Yes. The kind who want something badly, and then discover that the price they have paid for it is too high."

"So you don't think he was an out-and-out villain?"

"No; oh, no. Villains don't suffer, and that face is full of the most dreadful pain."

They considered the portrait in silence for a moment or two.

"It must have seemed like retribution, you know. Losing his only boy so soon after. And his wife's death. Being stripped of his own personal world in so short a time. It must have seemed like Divine justice."

"Would he care about his wife?"

"She was his cousin, and they had known each other from childhood. So whether he loved her or not, she must have been a companion for him. When you sit on a throne I suspect that companionship is a rare blessing. Now I must go and see how my hospital is getting on. I have not even asked the question that I came to ask. Which was how you felt this morning. But it is a very healthy sign that you have interest to spare for a man dead these four hundred years."

She had not moved from the position in which he had first caught sight of her. Now she smiled her faint, withdrawn smile, and with her hands still clasped lightly in front of her belt-buckle moved towards the door. She had a transcendental repose. Like a nun. Like a queen.

CHAPTER FOUR

It was after luncheon before Sergeant Williams reappeared, breathless, bearing two fat volumes.

"You should have left them with the porter," Grant said. "I didn't mean you to come sweating up here with them."

"I had to come up and explain. I had only time to go to one shop, but it's the biggest in the street. That's the best history of England they have in stock. It's the best there is anywhere, they say." He laid down a severe-looking sage-green tome, with an air of taking no responsibility for it. "They had no separate history of Richard III. I mean, no life of him. But they gave me this." This was a gay affair with a coat of arms on the wrapper. It was called *The Rose of Raby*.

"What is this?"

"She was his mother, it seems. The Rose in question, I mean. I can't wait: I'm due at the Yard in five minutes from now and the Super will flay me alive if I'm late. Sorry I couldn't do better. I'll look in again, first time I'm passing, and if these are no good I'll see what else I can get."

Grant was grateful and said so.

To the sound of Williams' brisk departing footsteps he began his inspection of the "best history of England there is." It turned out to be what is known as a "constitutional" history; a sober compilation lightened with improving illustrations. An illumination from the Luttrell Psalter decorated the husbandry of the fourteenth century, and a contemporary map of London bisected the Great

Fire. Kings and queens were mentioned only incidentally. Tanner's Constitutional History was concerned only with social progress and political evolution; with the Black Death, and the invention of printing, and the use of gunpowder, and the formation of the Trade Guilds, and so forth. But here and there Mr. Tanner was forced, by a horrid germaneness, to mention a king or his relations. And one such germaneness occurred in connection with the invention of printing.

A man called Caxton came out of the Weald of Kent as draper's apprentice to a future Lord Mayor of London, and then went to Bruges with the twenty marks his master left him in his will. And when, in the dreary autumn rain of the Low Countries, two young refugees from England fetched up on those low shores, in very low water, it was the successful merchant from the Weald of Kent who gave them succour. The refugees were Edward IV and his brother Richard; and when in the turn of the wheel Edward came back to rule England, Caxton came too, and the first books printed in England were printed for Edward IV and written by Edward's brother-in-law.

He turned the pages and marvelled how dull information is deprived of personality. The sorrows of humanity are no one's sorrows, as newspaper readers long ago found out. A *frisson* of horror may go down one's spine at wholesale destruction but one's heart stays unmoved. A thousand people drowned in floods in China are news: a solitary child drowned in a pond is tragedy. So Mr. Tanner's account of the progress of the English race was admirable but unexciting. But here and there where he could not avoid the personal his narrative flowered into a more immediate interest. In extracts from the Pastons' letters, for instance. The Pastons had a habit of sandwiching scraps of history between orders for salad oil and inquiries as to how Clement was doing at Cambridge. And between two of those domesticities appeared the small item that the two little York boys, George and Richard, were living in the Pastons' London lodgings, and that their brother Edward came every day to see them.

Surely, thought Grant, dropping the book for a moment on the counterpane and staring up at the now invisible ceiling, surely never before can anyone have come to the throne of England with so personal an experience of the ordinary man's life as Edward IV and his brother Richard. And perhaps only Charles II after them. And Charles, even in poverty and flight, had always been a King's son, a man apart. The two little boys who were living in the Pastons' lodgings were merely the babies of the York family. Of no particular importance at the best of times, and at the moment when the Pastons' letter was written without a home and possibly without a future.

Grant reached for The Amazon's history book to find out what Edward was about in London at that date, and learned that he was collecting an army. "London was always Yorkist in temper, and men flocked with enthusiasm to the banner of the youthful Edward," said the history book.

And yet young Edward, aged eighteen, idol of a captial city and on the way to the first of his victories, found time to come every day to see his small brothers.

Was it now, Grant wondered, that the remarkable devotion of Richard to his elder brother was born. An unwavering life-long devotion that the history books not only did not deny but actually used in order to point the moral. "Up to the moment of his brother's death Richard had been in all vicissitudes his loyal and faithful helpmeet, but the opportunity of a crown proved too much for him." Or in the simpler words of the Historical Reader: "He had been a good brother to Edward but when he saw that he might become King greed hardened his heart."

Grant took a sideways look at the portrait and decided that the Historical Reader was off the beam. Whatever had hardened Richard's heart to the point of murder had not been greed. Or did the Historical Reader mean greed for power? Probably. Probably.

But surely Richard must have had all the power that mortal man could wish. He was the King's brother, and rich. Was that short step further so important that he could murder his brother's children to achieve it?

It was an odd set-up altogether.

He was still mulling it over in his mind when Mrs. Tinker came in with fresh pyjamas for him and her daily précis of the newspaper headlines. Mrs. Tinker never read past the third headline of a report unless it happened to be a murder, in which case she read every word and bought an evening paper for herself on the way home to cook Tinker's supper.

Today the gentle burble of her comment on a Yorkshire arsenic-and-exhumation case flowed over him unbroken until she caught sight of the morning paper lying in its virgin condition alongside the books on the table. This brought her to a sudden halt.

"You not feelin' so good today?" she asked in a concerned way.

"I'm fine, Tink, fine. Why?"

"You 'aven't as much as opened your paper. That's 'ow my sister's gel started her decline. Not takin' no notice of what was in the paper."

"Don't worry. I'm on the up-grade. Even my temper has improved. I forgot about the paper because I've been reading history stories. Ever heard of the Princes in the Tower?"

"*Everyone's* 'eard of the Princes in the Tower."

"And do you know how they met their end?"

"Course I do. He put a pillow on their faces when they was asleep."

"Who did?"

"Their wicked uncle. Richard the Third. You didn't ought to think of things like that when you're poorly. You ought to be reading something nice and cheerful."

"Are you in a hurry to get home, Tink, or could you go round by St. Martin's Lane for me?"

"No, I've plenty of time. Is it Miss Hallard? She won't be at the theatre till six-about."

"No, I know. But you might leave a note for her and she'll get it when she comes in."

He reached for his scribbling pad and pencil and wrote:

"For the love of Mike find me a copy of Thomas More's History of Richard III."

He tore off the page, folded it and scribbled Marta's name on it.

"You can give it to old Saxton at the stage-door. He'll see that she gets it."

"If I can get near the stage-door what with the stools for the queue," Mrs. Tinker said; in comment rather than in truth. "That thing's going to run for ever."

She put the folded paper carefully away in the cheap pseudo-leather handbag with the shabby edges that was as much a part of her as her hat. Grant had, Christmas by Christmas, provided her with a new bag; each of them a work of art in the best tradition of English leather-working, an article so admirable in design and so perfect in execution that Marta Hallard might have carried it to luncheon at the Blague. But that was the last he had ever seen of any of them. Since Mrs. Tinker regarded a pawn-shop as one degree more disgraceful than prison, he absolved her from any suspicion of cashing in on her presents. He deduced that the handbags were safely laid away in a drawer somewhere, still wrapped up in the original tissue paper. Perhaps she took them out to show people sometimes, sometimes perhaps just to gloat over; or perhaps the knowledge that they were there enriched her, as the knowledge of "something put by for my funeral" might enrich another. Next Christmas he was going to open this shabby sack of hers, this perennial satchel *à toute faire*, and put something in the money compartment. She would fritter it away, of course, in small unimportances; so that in the end she would not know what she had done with it; but perhaps a series of small satisfactions scattered like sequins over the texture of everyday life was of greater worth than the academic satisfaction of owning a collection of fine objects at the back of a drawer.

When she had gone creaking away, in a shoes-and-corset concerto, he went back to Mr. Tanner and tried to improve his mind by acquiring some of Mr. Tanner's interest in the human race. But he found it an effort. Neither by nature nor by profession was he interested in mankind in the large. His bias, native and acquired, was towards the personal. He waded through Mr. Tanner's statistics and longed for a king in an oak tree, or a broom tied to a mast-head, or a Highlander hanging on to a trooper's stir-rup in a charge. But at least he had the satisfaction of learning that the Englishman of the fifteenth century "drank water only as a penance." The English labourer of Richard III's day was, it seemed, the admiration of the continent. Mr. Tanner quoted a contemporary, writing in France.

The King of France will allow no one to use salt, but what is bought of himself at his own arbitrary price. The troops pay for nothing, and treat the people barbarously if they are not satisfied. All growers of vines must give a fourth to the King. All the towns must pay the King great yearly sums for his men-at-arms. The peasants live in great hardship and misery. They wear no woollen. Their clothing consists of little short jerkins of sackcloth, no trowse but from the knees up, and legs exposed and naked. The women all go barefoot. The people eat no meat, except the fat of bacon in their soup. Nor are the gentry much better off. If an accusation is brought against them they are examined in private, and perhaps never more heard of.

In England it is very different. No one can abide in another man's house without his leave. The King cannot put on taxes, nor alter the laws, nor make new ones. The English never drink water except for penance. They eat all sorts of flesh and fish. They are clothed throughout in good woollens, and are provided with all sorts of household goods. An Englishman cannot be sued except before the ordinary judge.

And it seemed to Grant that if you were very hard up and wanted to go to see what your Lizzie's first-born looked like it must have been reassuring to know that there was shelter and a hand-out at every religious house, instead of wondering how you were going to raise the train fare. That green England he had fallen asleep with last night had a lot to be said for it.

He thumbed through the pages on the fifteenth century, looking for personal items; for individual reports that might, in their single vividness, illumine the scene for him as a "spot" lights the desired part of a stage. But the story was distressingly devoted to the general. According to Mr. Tanner, Richard III's only Parliament was the most liberal and progressive within record; and he regretted, did the worthy Mr. Tanner, that his private crimes should have militated against his patent desire for the common

43

weal. And that seemed to be all that Mr. Tanner had to say about Richard III. Except for the Pastons, chatting indestructibly through the centuries, there was a dearth of human beings in this record of humanity.

He let the book slide off his chest, and searched with his hand until he found *The Rose of Raby*.

CHAPTER FIVE

The *Rose of Raby* proved to be fiction, but it was at least easier to hold than Tanner's Constitutional History of England. It was, moreover, the almost-respectable form of historical fiction which is merely history-with-conversation, so to speak. An imaginative biography rather than an imagined story. Evelyn Payne-Ellis, whoever she might be, had provided portraits and a family tree, and had made no attempt, it seemed, to what he and his cousin Laura used to call in their childhood "write forsoothly." There were no "by our Ladys," no "nathelesses" or "varlets." It was an honest affair according to its lights.

And its lights were more illuminating than Mr. Tanner.

Much more illuminating.

It was Grant's belief that if you could not find out about a man, the next best way to arrive at an estimate of him was to find out about his mother.

So until Marta could provide him with the sainted and infallible Thomas More's personal account of Richard, he would do very happily with Cicely Nevill, Duchess of York.

He glanced at the family tree, and thought that if the two York brothers, Edward and Richard, were, as kings, unique in their experience of ordinary life they were no less unique in their Englishness. He looked at their breeding and marvelled. Nevill, Fitzalan, Percy, Holland, Mortimer, Clifford and Audley, as well as Plantagenet. Queen Elizabeth (who made it her boast) was all English; if one counted the Welsh streak as English. But among all the half-bred monarchs who had graced the throne between the Conquest and Farmer George—half-French, half-Spanish, half-Danish, half-Dutch, half-Portuguese—Edward IV and Richard III were remarkable in their home-bred quality.

They were also, he noted, as royally bred on their mother's side as on their father's. Cicely Nevill's grandfather was John of Gaunt, the first of the Lancasters; third son of Edward III. Her husband's two grandfathers were two other sons of Edward III. So three of Edward III's five sons had contributed to the making of the two York brothers.

"To be a Nevill" said Miss Payne-Ellis "was to be of some importance since they were great landowners. To be a Nevill was almost certainly to be handsome, since they were a good-looking family. To be a Nevill was to have personality, since they excelled in displays of both character and temperament. To unite all three Nevill gifts, in their finest quality, in one person was the good fortune of Cicely Nevill, who was the sole Rose of the north long before that north was forced to choose between White Roses and Red."

It was Miss Payne-Ellis's contention that the marriage with Richard Plantagenet, Duke of York, was a love match. Grant received this theory with a scepticism bordering on scorn until he noticed the results of that marriage. To have a yearly addition to the family was not, in the fifteenth century, evidence of anything but fertility. And the long family produced by Cicely Nevill to her charming husband augured nothing nearer love than cohabitation. But in a time when the wife's rôle was to stay meekly at home and see to her still-room, Cecily Nevill's constant travellings about in her husband's company were surely remarkable enough to suggest an abnormal pleasure in that company. The extent and constancy of that travel was witnessed to by the birthplaces of her children. Anne, her first, was born at Fotheringhay, the family home in Northamptonshire. Henry, who died as a baby, at Hatfield. Edward at Rouen, where the Duke was on active service. Edmund and Elizabeth also at Rouen. Margaret at Fotheringhay. John, who died young, at

Neath in Wales. George in Dublin (and could it be, wondered Grant, that that accounted for the almost Irish perverseness of the ineffable George?). Richard at Fotheringhay.

Cicely Nevill had not sat at home in Northamptonshire waiting for her lord and master to visit her when it seemed good to him. She had accompanied him about the world of their inhabiting. There was a strong presumption in favour of Miss Payne-Ellis's theory. At the very canniest reckoning it was patently a very successful marriage.

Which perhaps accounted for the family devotion of those daily visits of Edward to his small brothers in the Pastons' lodgings. The York family, even before tribulations, was a united one.

This was borne out unexpectedly when, spurting the pages from under his thumb, he came on a letter. It was a letter from the two elder boys, Edward and Edmund, to their father. The boys were at Ludlow Castle, undergoing their education, and on a Saturday in Easter week, taking advantage of a courier who was going back, they burst out in loud complaint of their tutor and his "odiousness" and begged their father to listen to the tale of the courier, William Smyth, who was fully charged with the details of their oppression. This S.O.S was introduced and ended in respectful padding, the formality of which was a little marred by their pointing out that it was nice of him to send the clothes but that he had forgotten their breviary.

The conscientious Miss Payne-Ellis had given the reference for this letter (one of the Cotton manuscripts, it appeared) and he thumbed more slowly, in search of more. Factual evidence was a policeman's meat.

He could not find any, but he came on a family tableau which held him for a moment.

The Duchess moved out into the thin sharp sunlight of a London December morning, and stood on the steps to watch them go: her husband, her brother, and her son. Dirk and his nephews brought the horses into the courtyard, scattering the pigeons and the fussing sparrows from the cobbles. She watched her husband mount, equable and deliberate as always, and thought that for all the emotion he showed he might be riding

47

down to Fotheringhay to look at some new rams instead of setting out on a campaign. Salisbury, her brother, was being Nevill and temperamental; a little conscious of the occasion and living up to it. She looked at them both and smiled in her mind at them. But it was Edmund who caught at her heart. Edmund at seventeen, very slender, very untried, very vulnerable. Flushed with pride and excitement at this setting-out to his first campaigning. She wanted to say to her husband: "Take care of Edmund," but she could not do that. Her husband would not understand; and Edmund, if he were to suspect, would be furious. If Edward, only a year older, was commanding an army of his own on the borders of Wales at this very minute, then he, Edmund, was more than old enough to see a war at first-hand.

She glanced behind her at the three younger children who had come out in her wake; Margaret and George, the two solid fair ones, and behind them, a pace in the rear as always, her changeling baby, Richard; his dark brows and brown hair making him look like a visitor. Good-natured untidy Margaret watched with all the moist-eyed emotion of fourteen; George in a passionate envy and wild rebellion that he was only eleven and of no consequence in this martial moment. Thin little Richard showed no excitement at all, but his mother thought that he vibrated like a softly tapped drum.

The three horses moved out of the courtyard in a clatter of slipping hooves and jingling accoutrements, to join the servants waiting for them in the roadway, and the children called and danced and waved them out of the gate.

And Cicely, who in her time had seen so many men, and so many of her family, go off to war, went back to the house with an unaccustomed weight at her bosom. Which of them, said the voice in her unwilling mind, which of them was it who was not coming back?

Her imagination did not compass anything so horrible as the fact that none of them was coming back again. That she would never see any one of them again.

That before the year was ended her husband's severed head, crowned for insult with a paper crown, would be nailed above the Micklegate Bar in York, and the heads of her brother and her son on the two other gates.

Well, that might be fiction, but it was an illuminating glimpse of Richard. The dark one in a blond family. The one who "looked like a visitor." The "changeling."

He abandoned Cicely Nevill for the moment, and went hunting through the book for her son Richard. But Miss Payne-Ellis seemed not to be greatly interested in Richard. He was merely the tail-end of the family. The magnificent young creature who flourished at the other end was more to her taste. Edward was much to the fore. With his Nevill cousin Warwick, Salisbury's son, he won the battle of Towton, and, with the memory of Lancastrian ferocity still fresh and his father's head still nailed to the Micklegate Bar, gave evidence of that tolerance that was to be characteristic of him. There was quarter at Towton for all who asked. He was crowned King of England in Westminster Abbey (and two small boys, home from exile in Utrecht, were created respectively Duke of Clarence and Duke of Gloucester). And he buried his father and his brother Edmund with great magnificence in the church at Fotheringhay (though it was Richard, aged thirteen, who convoyed that sad procession from Yorkshire, through the bright glory of five July days, to Northamptonshire; nearly six years after he had stood on the steps of Baynard's Castle in London to watch them ride away).

It was not until Edward had been King for some time that Miss Payne-Ellis allowed Richard to come back into the story. He was then being educated with his Nevill cousins at Middleham, in Yorkshire.

As Richard rode into the shadow of the keep, out of the broad sunlight and flying winds of Wensleydale, it seemed to him that there was an atmosphere of strangeness about the place. The guards were talking in loud excitement in the gatehouse and seemed abashed at his presence. From their sudden silence he rode on into a silent court that should have been bustling with activity at this hour of the day. It would soon be supper time, and both habit and hunger brought all the inhabitants of Middleham home from their various occupations, as they were bringing him back from his hawking, for the evening meal. This hush, this desertion, was unusual. He walked his horse to the stables, but there was no one there to give it to. As he unsaddled he noticed a hard-ridden bay in the next stall; a horse that did not belong to Middleham; a horse so tired that he had not eaten up and his head hung in a despondent beaten way between his knees.

Richard wiped his horse down and rugged him, brought him some hay and fresh water, and left him; wondering about that beaten horse and the uncanny silence. As he paused in the doorway he could hear voices in the distance of the great hall; and debated whether he should go there and investigate before going upstairs to his own quarters. As he hesitated a voice from the stairs above him said: "Z-z-zt!"

He looked up to see his cousin Anne's head peering over the banisters, her two long fair plaits hanging down like bell-ropes.

"Richard!" she said, half whispering. "Have you heard?"

"Is something wrong?" he asked. "What is it?"

As he moved up to her she grabbed his hand and dragged him upwards towards their schoolroom in the roof.

"But what is it?" he asked, leaning back in protest against her urgency. "What has happened? Is it something so awful that you can't tell me here!"

She swept him into the schoolroom and shut the door.

"It's Edward!"

"Edward? Is he ill?"

"No! *Scandal!*"

"Oh," said Richard, relieved. Scandal and Edward were never far apart. "What is it? Has he a new mistress?"

"Much worse than that! Oh, much, *much* worse. He's married."

"Married?" said Richard, so unbelieving that he sounded calm. "He can't be."

"But he is. The news came from London an hour ago."

"He can't be married," Richard insisted. "For a King marriage is a long affair. A matter of contracts, and agreements. A matter for Parliament, even, I think. What made you think he had got married?"

"I don't *think*," Anne said, out of patience at this sober reception of her broadside. "The whole family is raging together in the Great Hall over the affair."

"Anne! have you been listening at the door?"

"Oh, don't be so righteous. I didn't have to listen very hard, anyhow. You could hear them on the other side of the river. He has married Lady Grey!"

"Who is Lady Grey? Lady Grey of Groby?"

"Yes."

"But he can't. She has two children and she's quite old."

"She is five years older than Edward, and she is wonderfully beautiful—so I overhear."

"When did this happen?"

"They've been married five months. They got married in secret down in Northamptonshire."

"But I thought he was going to marry the King of France's sister."

"So," said Anne in a tone full of meaning, "did my father."

"Yes; yes, it makes things very awkward for him, doesn't it; after all the negotiating."

"According to the messenger from London he is throwing fits. It isn't only the making him look a fool. It seems she has cohorts of relations and he hates every one of them."

"Edward must be possessed." In Richard's hero-worshipping eyes everything Edward did had always been right. This folly, this undeniable, this inexcusable folly, could come only from possession.

"It will break my mother's heart," he said. He thought of his mother's courage when his father and Edmund had been killed, and the Lancastrian army was almost at the gates of London. She had not wept nor wrapped herself in protective veils of self-pity. She had arranged that he and George should go to Utrecht, as if she were arranging for them to go away to school. They might never see each other again, but she had busied herself about warm clothes for their winter voyage across the Channel with a calm and dry-eyed practicality.

How would she bear this; this further blow? This destructive folly. This shattering foolishness.

"Yes," said Anne, softening. "Poor Aunt Cicely. It is monstrous of Edward to hurt everyone so. Monstrous."

But Edward was still the infallible. If Edward had done wrong it was because he was ill, or possessed, or bewitched. Edward still had Richard's allegiance; his heart-whole and worshipping allegiance.

Nor in after years was that allegiance—an adult allegiance of recognition and acceptance—ever less than heart-whole.

And then the story went on to Cicely Nevill's tribulation, and her efforts to bring some kind of order into the relations between her son Edward, half-pleased, half-ashamed, and her nephew Warwick, wholly furious. There was also a long description of that indestructibly virtuous beauty with the famous "gilt" hair, who had succeeded where more complaisant beauties had failed; and of her enthroning at Reading Abbey (led to the throne by a silently protesting Warwick, who could not but note the large array of Woodvilles, come to see their sister Elizabeth acknowledged Queen of England).

The next time Richard turned up in the tale he was setting out from Lynn without a penny in his pocket, in a Dutch vessel that happened to be in the harbour when it was needed. Along with him was his brother Edward, Edward's friend Lord Hastings, and a few followers. None of them had anything except what they stood up in, and after some argument the ship's captain agreed to accept Edward's fur-lined cape as fare.

Warwick had finally decided that the Woodville clan was more than he could stomach. He had helped to put his cousin Edward on the throne of England; he could just as easily unseat him. For the achievement of this he had the help of the whole Nevill brood; and, incredibly, the active assistance of the ineffable George. Who had decided that falling heir to half the lands of Montague, Nevill, and Beauchamp, by marrying Warwick's other daughter Isabel, was a better bet than being loyal to his brother Edward. In eleven days Warwick was master of a surprised England, and Edward and Richard were squelching through the October mud between Alkmaar and The Hague.

From then on, Richard was always in the background of the story. Through that dreary winter in Bruges. Staying with Margaret in Burgundy—for that kind moist-eyed Margaret who had stood on the steps of Baynard's Castle with himself and George to watch their father ride away was now the very new Duchess of Burgundy. Margaret, kind Margaret, was saddened and dismayed—as many people in future were to be saddened and dismayed—by George's inexplicable conduct, and set herself to missionary work what time she got together funds for her two more admirable brothers.

Not even Miss Payne-Ellis's interest in the magnificent Edward allowed her to conceal that the real work of outfitting the ships hired with Margaret's money was done by Richard; a Richard not yet eighteen. And when Edward with an absurd handful of followers found himself once more camped in an English meadow, facing George with an army, it was Richard who went over to George's camp and talked the Margaret-weakened George into alliance again and so left the road to London open to them.

Not, Grant thought, that this last was any great achievement. George could obviously be talked into anything. He was the born missionee.

CHAPTER SIX

He had not nearly exhausted *The Rose of Raby* and the illicit joys of fiction when, next morning about eleven, a parcel arrived from Marta containing the more respectable entertainment of history as recorded by the sainted Sir Thomas.

With the book was a note in Marta's large sprawling writing on Marta's stiff expensive notepaper.

Have to send this instead of bringing it. Frantically busy. Think I have got M.M. to the sticking point re Blessington. No T. More in any of the bookshops, so tried Public Library. Can't think why one never thinks of Public Libraries. Probably because books expected to be soupy. Think this looks quite clean and unsoupy. You get fourteen days. Sounds like a sentence rather than a loan. Hope this interest in Crouchback means that the prickles are less nettlish. Till soon.

Marta.

The book did indeed look clean and unsoupy, if a little elderly. But after the light going of *The Rose* its print looked unexciting and its solid paragraphs forbidding. Nevertheless he attacked it with interest. This was, after all, where Richard III was concerned, "the horse's mouth."

He came to the surface an hour later, vaguely puzzled and ill at ease. It was not that the matter surprised him; the facts were very much what he had expected them to be. It was that this was not how he had expected Sir Thomas to write.

He took ill rest at nights, lay long waking and musing; sore wearied with care and watch, he slumbered rather than slept. So was his restless heart continually tossed and tumbled with the tedious impression and stormy remembrance of his most abominable deeds.

That was all right. But when he added that "this he had from such as were secret with his chamberers" one was suddenly repelled. An aroma of back-stair gossip and servants' spying came off the page. So that one's sympathy tilted before one was aware of it from the smug commentator to the tortured creature sleepless on his bed. The murderer seemed of greater stature than the man who was writing of him.

Which was all wrong.

Grant was conscious too of the same unease that filled him when he listened to a witness telling a perfect story that he knew to be flawed somewhere.

And that was very puzzling indeed. What could possibly be wrong with the personal account of a man revered for his integrity as Thomas More had been revered for four centuries?

The Richard who appeared in More's account was, Grant thought, one that Matron would have recognised. A man highly-strung and capable of both great evil and great suffering. "He was never quiet in his mind, never thought himself secure. His eyes whirled about, his body was privily fenced, his hand ever on his dagger, his countenance and manner like one always ready to strike again."

And of course there was the dramatic, not to say hysterical, scene that Grant remembered from his schooldays; that every schoolboy probably remembered. The council scene in the Tower before he laid claim to the crown. Richard's sudden challenge to Hastings as to what was the proper fate for a man who plotted the death of the Protector of the Kingdom. The insane claim that Edward's wife and Edward's mistress (Jane Shore) were responsible for his withered arm by their sorcery. The smiting of the table in his rage, which was the signal for his armed satellites to burst in and arrest Lord Hastings, Lord Stanley, and John Morton, Bishop of Ely. The rushing of Hastings down into the courtyard and his beheading on a handy log of wood after bare time to confess himself to the first priest who could be found.

That was certainly the picture of a man who would act first—in fury, in fear, in revenge—and repent afterwards.

But it seemed that he was capable of more calculated iniquity. He caused a sermon to be preached by a certain Dr. Shaw, brother of the Lord Mayor, at Paul's Cross, on June 22, on the text: "Bastard slips shall take no root." Wherein Dr. Shaw maintained that both Edward and George were sons of the Duchess of York by some unknown man, and that Richard was the only legitimate son of the Duke and Duchess of York.

This was so unlikely, so inherently absurd, that Grant went back and read it over again. But it still said the same thing. That Richard had traduced his mother, in public and for his own material advantage, with an unbelievable infamy.

Well, Sir Thomas More said it. And if anyone should know it would be Thomas More. And if anyone should know how to pick and choose between the credibilities in the reporting of a story it ought to be Thomas More, Lord Chancellor of England.

Richard's mother, said Sir Thomas, complained bitterly of the slander with which her son had smirched her. Understandably, on the whole, Grant thought.

As for Dr. Shaw, he was overcome with remorse. So much so that "within a few days he withered and consumed away."

Had a stroke, probably, Grant considered. And little wonder. To have stood up and told that tale to a London crowd must have taken some nerve.

Sir Thomas's account of the Princes in the Tower was the same as The Amazon's, but Sir Thomas's version was more detailed. Richard had suggested to Robert Brackenbury, Constable of the Tower, that it might be a good thing if the Princes disappeared, but Brackenbury would have no part in such an act. Richard therefore waited until he was at Warwick, during his progress through England after his coronation, and then sent Tyrrel to London with orders that he was to receive the keys of the Tower for one night. During that night two ruffians, Dighton and Forrest, one a groom and one a warder, smothered the two boys.

At this point The Midget came in with his lunch and removed the book from his grasp; and while he forked the shepherd's pie from plate to mouth he considered again the face of the man in the dock. The faithful and patient small brother who had turned into a monster.

When The Midget came back for his tray he said: "Did you know that Richard III was a very popular person in his day? Before he came to the throne, I mean."

The Midget cast a baleful glance at the picture.

"Always was a snake in the grass, if you ask me. Smooth, that's what he was: smooth. Biding his time."

Biding his time for what? he wondered, as she tapped away down the corridor. He could not have known that his brother Edward would die unexpectedly at the early age of forty. He could not have foreseen (even after a childhood shared with him in uncommon intimacy) that George's ongoings would end in attainder and the debarring of his two children from the succession. There seemed little point in "biding one's time" if there was nothing to bide for. The indestructibly virtuous beauty with the gilt hair had, except for her incurable nepotism, proved an admirable Queen and had provided Edward with a large brood of healthy children, including two boys. The whole of that brood, together with George and his son and daughter, stood between Richard and the throne. It was surely unlikely that a man busy with the administration of the North of England, or campaigning (with dazzling success) against the Scots, would have much spare interest in being "smooth."

What then had changed him so fundamentally in so short a time?

Grant reached for *The Rose of Raby* to see what Miss Payne-Ellis had had to say about the unhappy metamorphosis of Cicely Nevill's youngest son. But that wily author had burked the issue. She had wanted the book to be a happy one, and to have carried it to its logical conclusion would have made it unredeemed tragedy. She had therefore wound it up with a fine resounding major chord by making her last chapter the coming-out of young Elizabeth, Edward's eldest child. This avoided both the tragedy of Elizabeth's young brothers and the defeat and death of Richard in battle.

So the book ended with a Palace party, and a flushed and happy young Elizabeth, very magnificent in a new white dress and her first pearls, dancing the soles out of her slippers like the princesses in the fairy-tale. Richard and Anne, and their delicate little son, had come up from Middleham for the occasion. But neither George nor Isabel was there. Isabel had died in childbirth years ago, obscurely and as far as George was concerned unmourned. George too had died obscurely, but with that perverseness that was so peculiarly George's, had by that very obscurity won for himself imperishable fame.

George's life had been a progression from one spectacular piece of spiritual extravagance to the next. Each time, his family must have said: Well, that at last is the summit of frightfulness; even George cannot think of anything more fantastic than that. And each time George had surprised them. There was no limit to George's antic capacity.

The seed was perhaps sown when, during his first backsliding in the company of his father-in-law, Warwick had created him heir to the poor crazy puppet-King, Henry VI, whom Warwick had dumped back on the throne to spite his cousin Edward. Both Warwick's hopes of seeing his daughter a Queen and George's royal pretensions had gone down the drain on that night when Richard had gone over to the Lancastrian camp and talked to George. But the taste of importance had perhaps proved too much for a natural sweet-tooth. In the years to come the family were always heading George off from unexpected vagaries, or rescuing him from his latest caper.

When Isabel died he had been certain that she had been poisoned by her waiting woman, and that his baby son had been poisoned by another. Edward, thinking the affair important enough to be tried before a London court, sent down a writ; only to find that George had tried them both at a petty sessions of his own magistrates and hanged them. The furious Edward, by way of rapping him over the knuckles, had two members of George's household tried for treason; but instead of taking the hint George declared that this was just judicial murder, and went about saying so in loud tones and a fine blaze of *lèse-majesté*.

Then he decided that he wanted to marry the richest heiress in Europe; who was Margaret's step-daughter, young Mary of Burgundy. Kind Margaret thought that it would be nice to have her brother in Burgundy, but Edward had arranged to back Maximilian of Austria's suit, and George was a continual embarrassment.

When the Burgundy intrigue came to nothing, the family hoped for a little peace. After all, George owned half the Nevill lands and had no need to marry again either for fortune or children. But George had a new scheme for marrying Margaret, the sister of James III of Scotland.

At last his *folie de grandeur* graduated from secret negotiation undertaken on his own behalf with foreign courts to open display of the Lancastrian act of Parliament which had declared him heir to the throne after Henry VI. This, inevitably, landed him before another Parliament, and a much less amenable one.

The trial was chiefly remarkable for a flaming and wordy row between the two brothers, Edward and George, but when the expected attainder was passed, there was a pause. Depriving George of his standing was one thing: desirable and indeed necessary. But executing him was something else again.

As the days went by without sentence being carried out, the Commons sent a reminder. And next day it was announced that George, Duke of Clarence, had died in the Tower.

"Drowned in a butt of malmsey," said London. And what was merely a Cockney's comment on a drunkard's end passed into history and made the undeserving George immortal.

So George was not at that party at Westminster, and the emphasis in Miss Payne-Ellis's final chapter was not on Cicely Nevill as the mother of sons, but on Cicely Nevill the grandmother of a fine brood. George might have died discredited, on a dried-leaf heap of worn-out friendships, but his son, young Warwick, was a fine upstanding boy, and little Margaret at ten was already showing signs of the traditional Nevill beauty. Edmund, dead in battle at seventeen, might seem a wanton waste of young life, but there to balance it was the delicate baby whom she had never thought to rear; and he had a son to follow him. Richard in his twenties still looked as though one could break him in two, but he was as tough as a heather root, and perhaps his fragile-looking son would grow up to be as resilient. As for Edward, her tall blond Edward, his beauty might be blurring into grossness and his amiability into sloth, but his two small sons and his five girls had all the character and good looks of their combined ancestry.

As a grandmother she could look on that crowd of children with a personal pride, and as a Princess of England she could look on them with assurance. The crown was safe in the York line for generations to come.

If anyone, looking in a crystal ball at that party, had told Cicely Nevill that in four years not only the York line but the whole Plantagenet dynasty would have gone for ever, she would have held it to be either madness or treason.

But what Miss Payne-Ellis had not sought to gloss over was the prevalence of the Woodville clan in a Nevill-Plantagenet gathering.

She looked round the room and wished that her daughter-in-law Elizabeth had been blessed either with a less generous heart or with fewer relations. The Woodville match had turned out far more happily than anyone had dared to hope; Elizabeth had been an admirable wife; but the by-products had not been so fortunate. It was perhaps inevitable that the governorship of the two boys should have gone to her eldest brother; and Rivers, if a little nouveau riche in his liking for display and a little too obviously ambitious, was a cultured creature and an admirable person to have the boys in charge during their school-room days at Ludlow. But as for the rest: four brothers, seven sisters, and two sons by her first husband, were really too many by half to have brought into the marriage market in her wake.

Cicely looked across the laughing mêlée of the children's blind man's buff to the grown-ups standing round the supper table. Anne Woodville married to the Earl of Essex's heir. Eleanor Woodville married to the Earl of Kent's heir. Margaret Woodville married to the Earl of Arundel's heir. Catherine Woodville married to the Duke of Buckingham. Jacquette Woodville to Lord Strange. Mary Woodville to Lord Herbert's heir. And John Woodville, disgracefully, to the Dowager of Norfolk who was old enough to be his grandmother. It was good that new blood should strengthen the old families—new blood had always seeped in—but it was not good that it should come suddenly and in a flood from one particular source. It was like a fever in the political blood of the country; a foreign introduction, difficult to be assimilated. Unwise and regrettable.

However. There were long years ahead in which that influx could be assimilated. This new sudden power in the body politic would cease to be so concentrated, would spread out, would settle down, would cease to be dangerous and upsetting. Edward for all his amiability had a shrewd common sense; he would keep the country on an even keel as he had kept it for nearly twenty years. No one had run England with a more despotic power or a lighter hand than her acute, lazy, woman-loving Edward.

It would be all right eventually.

She was about to rise and join them in their discussion of sweetmeats—they must not think that she was being critical or aloof—when her granddaughter Elizabeth came breathless and laughing out of the scrimmage and swept into the seat beside her.

"I am much too old for this sort of thing," she said between her gasps, "and it is ruinous to one's clothes. Do you like my dress, grandmother? I had to coax it out of Father. He said my old tawny satin would do. The one I had when Aunt Margaret came from Burgundy to visit us. That is the worst of having a father who notices what women wear. He knows too much about one's wardrobe. Did you hear that the Dauphin has jilted me? Father is in a pet, but I am so happy. I lighted ten candles to St. Catherine. It took all I had left of my

61

allowance. I don't want to leave England. I want never to leave England ever. Can you arrange that for me, grandmother?"

Cicely smiled and said that she would try.

"Old Ankaret, who tells fortunes, says that I am to be a Queen. But since there is no prince to marry me I do not see how that may be." She paused, and added in a smaller voice: "She said Queen of England. But I expect she was just a little tipsy. She is very fond of hippocras."

It was unfair, not to say inartistic, of Miss Payne-Ellis to hint at Elizabeth's future as the wife of Henry VII if as author she was not prepared to face the unpleasantness that lay between. To presuppose in her readers a knowledge of Elizabeth's marriage to the first Tudor king, was also to presuppose their awareness of her brother's murder. So that a dark reminding shadow fell across the festive scene with which she had chosen to end her story.

But on the whole, Grant thought, she had made a good enough job of the story, judging by what he had read of it. He might even go back sometime and read the bits he had skipped.

CHAPTER SEVEN

Grant had switched off his bedside light that night, and was half asleep, when a voice in his mind said, "But Thomas More was Henry the Eighth."

This brought him wide awake. He flicked the light on again.

What the voice had meant, of course, was not that Thomas More and Henry the Eighth were one and the same person, but that, in that business of putting personalities into pigeon-holes according to reigns, Thomas More belonged to the reign of Henry the Eighth.

Grant lay looking at the pool of light that his lamp threw on the ceiling, and reckoned. If Thomas More was Henry VIII's Chancellor, then he must have lived through the whole of Henry VII's long reign as well as Richard III's. There was something wrong somewhere.

He reached for More's *History of Richard II*. It had as preface a short life of More which he had not bothered to read. Now he turned to it to find out how More could have been both Richard III's historian and Henry VIII's Chancellor. How old was More when Richard succeeded?

He was five.

When that dramatic council scene had taken place at the Tower, Thomas More had been five years old. He had been only eight when Richard died at Bosworth.

Everything in that history had been hearsay.

And if there was one word that a policeman loathed more than another it was hearsay. Especially when applied to evidence.

He was so disgusted that he flung the precious book on to the floor before he remembered that it was the property of a Public Library and his only by grace and for fourteen days.

More had never known Richard III at all. He had indeed grown up under a Tudor administration. That book was the Bible of the whole historical world on the subject of Richard III—it was from that account that Holinshed had taken his material, and from that that Shakespeare had written his—and except that More believed what he wrote to be true it was of no more value than what the soldier said. It was what his cousin Laura called "snow on their boots." A "gospel-true" event seen by someone other than the teller. That More had a critical mind and an admirable integrity did not make the story acceptable evidence. A great many otherwise admirable minds had accepted that story of the Russian troops passing through Britain. Grant had dealt too long with the human intelligence to accept as truth someone's report of someone's report of what that someone remembered to have seen or been told.

He was disgusted.

At the first opportunity he must get an actual contemporary account of the events of Richard's short reign. The Public Library could have Sir Thomas More back tomorrow and be damned to their fourteen days. The fact that Sir Thomas was a martyr and a Great Mind did not cut any ice at all with him, Alan Grant. He, Alan Grant, had known Great Minds so uncritical that they would believe a story that would make a con man blush for shame. He had known a great scientist who was convinced that a piece of butter muslin was his great-aunt Sophia because an illiterate medium from the back streets of Plymouth told him so. He had known a great authority on the Human Mind and Its Evolution who had been taken for all he had by an incurable knave because he "judged for himself and not on police stories." As far as he, Alan Grant, was concerned there was nothing so uncritical or so damn-silly as your Great Mind. As far as he, Alan Grant, was concerned Thomas More was washed out, cancelled, deleted; and he, Alan Grant, was beginning from scratch again tomorrow morning.

He was still illogically fuming when he fell asleep and he woke fuming.

"Do you know that your Sir Thomas More knew nothing about Richard III at all?" he said, accusing, to The Amazon the moment her large person appeared in the doorway.

She looked startled, not at his news but at his ferocity. Her eyes looked as if they might brim with tears at another rough word.

"But of *course* he knew!" she protested. "He *lived* then."

"He was eight when Richard died," Grant said, relentless. "And all he knew was what he had been told. Like me. Like you. Like Will Rogers of blessed memory. There is nothing hallowed at all about Sir Thomas More's history of Richard III. It's a damned piece of hearsay and a swindle."

"Aren't you feeling so well this morning?" she asked anxiously. "Do you think you've got a temperature?"

"I don't know about a temperature, but my blood pressure's away up."

"Oh dear, dear," she said, taking this literally. "And you were doing so very well. Nurse Ingham will be so distressed. She has been boasting about your good recovery."

That The Midget should have found him a subject for boasting was a new idea to Grant, but it was not one that gave him any gratification. He resolved to have a temperature in earnest if he could manage it, just to score off The Midget.

But the morning visit of Marta distracted him from this experiment in the power of mind over matter.

Marta, it seemed, was pluming herself on his mental health very much as The Midget was pluming herself on his physical improvement. She was delighted that her pokings-about with James in the print shop had been so effective.

"Have you decided on Perkin Warbeck, then?" she asked.

"No. Not Warbeck. Tell me: what made you bring me a portrait of Richard III? There's no mystery about Richard, is there?"

"No. I suppose we took it as illustration to the Warbeck story. No, wait a moment. I remember, James turned it up and said: 'If he's mad about faces, there's one for him!'

He said: 'That's the most notorious murderer in history, and yet his face is in my estimation the face of a saint.' "

"A saint!" Grant said; and then remembered something. " 'Over-conscientious,' " he said.

"What?"

"Nothing. I was just remembering my first impressions of it. Is that how it seemed to you: the face of a saint?"

She looked across to the picture, propped up against the pile of books. "I can't see it against the light," she said, and picked it up for a closer scrutiny.

He was suddenly reminded that to Marta, as to Sergeant Williams, faces were a professional matter. The slant of an eyebrow, the set of a mouth, was just as much an evidence of character to Marta as to Williams. Indeed she actually made herself faces to match the characters she played.

"Nurse Ingham thinks he's dreary. Nurse Darroll thinks he's a horror. My surgeon thinks he's a polio victim. Sergeant Williams thinks he's a born judge. Matron thinks he's a soul in torment."

Marta said nothing for a little. Then she said: "It's odd, you know. When you first look at it you think it a mean, suspicious face. Even cantankerous. But when you look at it a little longer you find that it isn't like that at all. It is quite calm. It is really quite a gentle face. Perhaps that is what James meant by being saint-like."

"No. No, I don't think so. What he meant was the subservience to conscience."

"Whatever it is, it *is a face*, isn't it! Not just a collection of organs for seeing, breathing, and eating with. A wonderful face. With very little alteration, you know, it might be a portrait of Lorenzo the Magnificent."

"You don't suppose that it *is* Lorenzo and that we're considering the wrong man altogether?"

"Of course not. Why should you think that?"

"Because nothing in the face fits the facts of history. And pictures have got shuffled before now."

"Oh, yes, of course they have. But that is Richard all right. The original—or what is supposed to be the original—is at Windsor Castle. James told me. It is included in Henry VIII's inventory, so it has been there for four hundred years or so. And there are duplicates at Hatfield and Albury."

"It's Richard," Grant said resignedly. "I just don't know anything about faces. Do you know anyone at the B.M.?"

"At the British Museum?" Marta asked, her attention still on the portrait. "No, I don't think so. Not that I can think of at the moment. I went there once to look at some Egyptian jewellery, when I was playing Cleopatra with Geoffrey—did you ever see Geoffrey's Antony? It was superlatively genteel—but the place frightens me rather. Such a garnering of the ages. It made me feel the way the stars make you feel: small and no-account. What do you want of the B.M.?"

"I wanted some information about history written in Richard III's day. Contemporary accounts."

"Isn't the sainted Sir Thomas any good, then?"

"The sainted Sir Thomas is nothing but an old gossip," Grant said with venom. He had taken a wild dislike to the much-admired More.

"Oh, dear. And the nice man at the Library seemed so reverent about him. The Gospel of Richard III according to St. Thomas More, and all that."

"Gospel nothing," Grant said rudely. "He was writing down in a Tudor England what someone had told him about events that happened in a Plantagenet England when he himself was five."

"Five years old?"

"Yes."

"Oh, dear. Not exactly the horse's mouth."

"Not even straight from the course. Come to think of it, it's as reliable as a bookie's tips would be. He's on the wrong side of the rails altogether. If he was a Tudor servant he was on the laying side where Richard III was concerned."

"Yes. Yes, I suppose so. What do you want to find out about Richard, when there is no mystery to investigate?"

"I want to know what made him tick. That is a more profound mystery than anything I have come up against of late. What changed him almost overnight? Up to the moment of his brother's death he seems to have been entirely

67

admirable. And devoted to his brother."

"I suppose the supreme honour must always be a temptation."

"He was Regent until the boy came of age. Protector of England. With his previous history, you would think that would have been enough for him. You would have thought, indeed, that it would have been very much his cup of tea: guardian of both Edward's son and the kingdom."

"Perhaps the brat was unbearable, and Richard longed to 'larn' him. Isn't it odd how we never think of victims as anything but white innocents. Like Joseph in the Bible. I'm sure he was a quite intolerable young man, actually, and long overdue for that pushing into the pit. Perhaps young Edward was just sitting up and begging to be quietly put down."

"There were two of them," Grant reminded her.

"Yes, of course. Of course there isn't an explanation. It was the ultimate barbarism. Poor little woolly lambs! Oh!"

"What was the 'Oh' for?"

"I've just thought of something. Woolly lambs made me think of it."

"Well?"

"No, I won't tell you in case it doesn't come off. I must fly."

"Have you charmed Madeleine March into agreeing to write the play?"

"Well, she hasn't actually signed a contract yet, but I think she is sold on the idea. Au revoir, my dear, I shall look in soon again."

She went away, sped on her way by a blushing Amazon, and Grant did not remember anything about woolly lambs until the woolly lamb actually turned up in his room next evening. The woolly lamb was wearing horn-rimmed spectacles, which in some odd way emphasized the resemblance instead of detracting from it. Grant had been dozing, more at peace with the world than he had been for some time; history was, as Matron had pointed out, an excellent way of acquiring a sense of perspective. The tap at his door was so tentative that he had decided that he had imagined it. Taps on hospital doors are not apt to be tentative. But something made him say: "Come in!" and there in the opening was something that was so unmistakably Marta's woolly lamb that Grant laughed aloud before he could stop himself.

The young man looked abashed, smiled nervously, propped the spectacles on his nose with a long thin forefinger, cleared his throat, and said:

"Mr. Grant? My name is Carradine. Brent Carradine. I hope I haven't disturbed you when you were resting."

"No, no. Come in, Mr. Carradine. I am delighted to see you."

"Marta—Miss Hallard, that is—sent me. She said I could be of some help to you."

"Did she say how? Do sit down. You'll find a chair over there behind the door. Bring it over."

He was a tall boy, hatless, with soft fair curls crowning a high forehead and a much too big tweed coat hanging unfastened round him in negligent folds, American-wise. Indeed, it was obvious that he was in fact American. He brought over the chair, planted himself on it with the coat spread round him like some royal robe and looked at Grant with kind brown eyes whose luminous charm not even the horn-rims could dim.

"Marta—Miss Hallard, that is—said that you wanted something looked up."

"And are you a looker-upper?"

"I'm doing research, here in London. Historical research, I mean. And she said something about your wanting something in that line. She knows I work at the B.M. most mornings. I'd be very pleased, Mr. Grant, to do anything I can to help you."

"That's very kind of you; very kind indeed. What is it that you are working on? Your research, I mean."

"The Peasants' Revolt."

"Oh, Richard II."

"Yes."

"Are you interested in social conditions?"

The young man grinned suddenly in a very unstudent-like way and said: "No, I'm interested in staying in England."

"And can't you stay in England without doing research?"

"Not very easily. I've got to have an alibi. My pop thinks I should go into the family business. It's furniture. Wholesale furniture. You order it by mail. Out of a book. Don't misunderstand me, Mr. Grant: it's very good furniture. Lasts for ever. It's just that I can't take much interest in furnishing-units."

"And, short of Polar exploration, the British Museum was the best hideaway you could think of."

"Well, it's warm. And I really do like history. I majored in it. And—well, Mr. Grant, if you really want to know, I just had to follow Atlanta Shergold to England. She's the dumb blonde in Marta's—I mean: in Miss Hallard's play. I mean she *plays* the dumb blonde. She's not at all dumb, Atlanta."

"No, indeed. A very gifted young woman indeed."

"You've seen her?"

"I shouldn't think there is anyone in London who hasn't seen her."

"No, I suppose not. It does go on and on, doesn't it? We didn't think—Atlanta and me—that it would run for more than a few weeks, so we just waved each other good-bye and said: See you at the beginning of the month! It was when we found that it was going on indefinitely that I just had to find an excuse to come to England."

"Wasn't Atlanta sufficient excuse?"

"Not for my pop! The family are very snooty about Atlanta, but Pop is the worst of the bunch. When he can bring himself to mention her he refers to her as 'that young actress acquaintance of yours.' You see, Pop is Carradine the Third, and Atlanta's father is very much Shergold the First. A little grocery store on Main Street, as a matter of fact. And the salt of the earth, in case you're interested. And of course Atlanta hadn't really done very much, back in the States. I mean, on the stage. This is her first big success. That is why she didn't want to break her contract and come back home. As a matter of fact it'll be quite a fight to get her back home at all. She says we never appreciated her."

"So you took to research."

"I had to think of something that I could do only in London, you see. And I had done some research at college. So the B.M. seemed to be what you call my cup of tea. I could enjoy myself and yet show my father that I was really working, both at the same time."

"Yes. It's as nice an alibi as ever I met with. Why the Peasants' Revolt, by the way?"

"Well, it's an interesting time. And I thought it would please Pop."

"Is *he* interested in social reform, then?"

"No, but he hates kings."

"Carradine the Third?"

"Yes, it's a laugh, isn't it? I wouldn't put it past him to have a crown in one of his safe deposit boxes. I bet he takes out the parcel every now and then and sneaks over to Grand Central and tries it on in the men's washroom. I'm afraid I'm tiring you, Mr. Grant; gabbing on about my own affairs like this. I didn't come for that. I came to—"

"Whatever you came for, you're manna straight from heaven. So relax, if you're not in a hurry."

"I'm never in a hurry," the young man said, unfolding his legs and laying them out in front of him. As he did it his feet, at the far extremity of his long limbs, touched the bedside table and shook the portrait of Richard III from its precarious position, so that it dropped to the floor.

"Oh, pardon me! That was careless of me. I haven't really got used to the length of my legs yet. You'd think a fellow would be used to his growth by twenty-two, wouldn't you?" He picked up the photograph, dusted it carefully with the cuff of his sleeve, and looked at it with interest. "Richardus III. Ang. Rex.," he read aloud.

"You're the first person to have noticed that background writing," Grant said.

"Well, I suppose it isn't visible unless you look into it. You're the first person I ever met who had a king for a pinup."

"No beauty, is he?"

"I don't know," said the boy slowly. "It's not a bad face, as faces go. I had a prof. at college who looked rather like him. He lived on bismuth and glasses of milk so he had a slightly jaundiced outlook on life, but he was the kindest creature imaginable. Is it about Richard that you wanted information?"

"Yes. Nothing very abstruse or difficult. Just to know

71

what the contemporary authority is."

"Well, that should be easy enough. It isn't very far from my own time. I mean my research period. Indeed, the modern authority for Richard II—Sir Cuthbert Oliphant—stretches over both. Have you read Oliphant?" Grant said that he had read nothing but school books and Sir Thomas More.

"More? Henry VIII's Chancellor?"

"Yes."

"I take it that that was a bit of special pleading!"

"It read to me more like a party pamphlet," Grant said, realising for the first time that that was the taste that had been left in his mouth. It had not read like a statesman's account; it had read like a party throw-away.

No, it had read like a columnist. Like a columnist who got his information below-stairs.

"Do you know anything about Richard III?"

"Nothing except that he croaked his nephews, and offered his kingdom for a horse. And that he had two stooges known as the Cat and the Rat."

"What!"

"You know: 'The Cat, the Rat, and Love Our Dog, Rule all England under a Hog.' "

"Yes, of course. I'd forgotten that. What does it mean, do you know?"

"No, I've no idea. I don't know that period very well. How did you get interested in Richard III?"

"Marta suggested that I should do some academic investigating, since I can't do any practical investigating for some time to come. And because I find faces interesting she brought me portraits of all the principals. Principals in the various mysteries she suggested, I mean. Richard got in more or less by accident, but he proved the biggest mystery of the lot."

"He did? In what way?"

"He is the author of the most revolting crime in history, and he has the face of a great judge; a great administrator. Moreover he was by all accounts an abnormally civilised and well-living creature. He actually *was* a good administrator, by the way. He governed the North of England and did it excellently. He was a good staff officer and a good soldier. And nothing is known against his private life. His brother, perhaps you know, was—bar Charles Ⅱ—our most wench-ridden royal product."

"Edward IV. Yes, I know. A six-foot hunk of male beauty. Perhaps Richard suffered from a resentment at the contrast. And that accounts for his willingness to blot out his brother's seed."

This was something that Grant had not thought of.

"You're suggesting that Richard had a suppressed hate for his brother?"

"Why suppressed?"

"Because even his worst detractors admit that he was devoted to Edward. They were together in everything from the time that Richard was twelve or thirteen. The other brother was no good to anyone. George."

"Who was George?"

"The Duke of Clarence."

"Oh. Him! Butt-of-malmsey Clarence."

"That's the one. So there were just the two of them—Edward and Richard, I mean. And there was a ten-year gap in their ages. Just the right difference for hero worship."

"If I were a hunchback," young Carradine said musingly, "I sure would hate a brother who took my credit and my women and my place in the sun."

"It's possible," Grant said after an interval. "It's the best explanation I've come on so far."

"It mightn't have been an overt thing at all, you know. It mightn't have even been a conscious thing. It may just have all boiled up in him when he saw the chance of a crown. He may have said—I mean his blood may have said: 'Here's my chance! All those years of fetching and carrying and standing one pace in the rear, and no thanks for them. Here's where I take my pay. Here's where I settle accounts.' "

Grant noticed that by sheer chance Carradine had used the same imagined description of Richard as Miss Payne-Ellis. Standing one pace in the rear. That is how the novelist had seen him, standing with the fair, solid Margaret and George, on the steps of Baynard's Castle watching their father go away to war. One pace in the rear, "as usual."

"That's very interesting, though, what you say about

73

Richard being apparently a good sort up to the time of the crime," Carradine said, propping one leg of his hornrims with a long forefinger in his characteristic gesture. "Makes him more of a person. That Shakespeare version of him, you know, that's just a caricature. Not a man at all. I'll be very pleased to do any investigating you want, Mr. Grant. It'll make a nice change from the peasants."

"The Cat and the Rat instead of John Ball and Wat Tyler."

"That's it."

"Well, it's very nice of you. I'd be glad of anything you can rake up. But at the moment all I pine for is a contemporary account of events. They must have been country-rocking events. I want to read a contemporary's account of them. Not what someone heard-tell about events that happened when he was five, and under another régime altogether."

"I'll find out who the contemporary historian is. Fabyan, perhaps. Or is he Henry VII? Anyway, I'll find out. And meanwhile perhaps you'd like a look at Oliphant. He's the modern authority on the period, or so I understand."

Grant said that he would be delighted to take a look at Sir Cuthbert.

"I'll drop him in when I'm passing tomorrow—I suppose it'll be all right if I leave him in the office for you?—and as soon as I find out about the contemporary writers I'll be in with the news. That suit you?"

Grant said that that was perfect.

Young Carradine went suddenly shy, reminding Grant of the woolly lamb which he had quite forgotten in the interest of this new approach to Richard. He said goodnight in a quiet smothered way, and ambled out of the room followed by the sweeping skirts of his topcoat.

Grant thought that, the Carradine fortune apart, Atlanta Shergold looked like being on a good thing.

CHAPTER EIGHT

"Well," said Marta, when she came again, "what did you think of my woolly lamb?"

"It was *very* kind of you to find him for me."

"I didn't have to find him. He's continually underfoot. He practically lives at the theatre. He must have seen *To Sea in a Bowl* five hundred times; when he isn't in Atlanta's dressing-room he's in front. I wish they'd get married, and then we might see less of him. They're not even living together, you know. It's all pure idyll." She dropped her "actress" voice for a moment and said: "They're rather sweet together. In some ways they are more like twins than lovers. They have that utter trust in each other; that dependence on the other half to make a proper whole. And they never have rows—or even quarrels, that I can see. An idyll, as I said. Was it Brent who brought you this?"

She poked the solid bulk of Oliphant with a doubtful finger.

"Yes, he left it with the porter for me."

"It looks very indigestible."

"A bit unappetising, let us say. It is quite easily digested once you have swallowed it. History for the student. Set out in detailed fact."

"Ugh!"

"At least I've discovered where the revered and sainted Sir Thomas More got his account of Richard."

"Yes? Where?"

"From one John Morton."

"Never heard of him."

"Neither did I, but that's our ignorance."

"Who was he?"

"He was Henry VII's Archbishop of Canterbury. And Richard's bitterest enemy."

If Marta had been capable of whistling, she would have whistled in comment.

"So *that* was the horse's mouth!" she said.

"That was the horse's mouth. And it is on that account of Richard that all the later ones were built. It is on that story that Holinshed fashioned his history, and on that story that Shakespeare fashioned his character."

"So it is the version of someone who hated Richard. I didn't know that. Why did the sainted Sir Thomas report Morton rather than someone else?"

"Whoever he reported, it would be a Tudor version. But he reported Morton, it seems, because he had been in Morton's household as a boy. And of course Morton had been very much 'on in the act,' so it was natural to write down the version of an eyewitness whose account he could have at first hand."

Marta poked her finger at Oliphant again. "Does your dull fat historian acknowledge that it is a biassed version?"

"Oliphant? Only by implication. He is, to be honest, in a sad muddle himself about Richard. On the same page he says that he was an admirable administrator and general, with an excellent reputation, staid and good-living, very popular by contrast with the Woodville upstarts (the Queen's relations) and that he was 'perfectly unscrupulous and ready to wade through any depth of bloodshed to the crown which lay within his grasp.' On one page he says grudgingly: 'There are reasons for supposing that he was not destitute of a conscience' and then on a later page reports More's picture of a man so tormented by his own deed that he could not sleep. And so on."

"Does your dull fat Oliphant prefer his roses red, then?"

"Oh, I don't think so. I don't think he is consciously Lancastrian. Though now that I think of it he *is* very tolerant of Henry VII's usurpation. I can't remember his saying anywhere, brutally, that Henry hadn't a vestige of a shadow of a claim to the throne."

76

"Who put him there, then? Henry, I mean."

"The Lancastrian remnant and the upstart Woodvilles, backed, I suppose, by a country revolted by the boys' murder. Apparently anyone with a spice of Lancastrian blood in their veins would do. Henry himself was canny enough to put 'conquest' first in his claim to the throne, and his Lancaster blood second, 'De jure belli et de jure Lancastriae.' His mother was the heir of an illegitimate son of the third son of Edward III."

"All I know about Henry VII is that he was fantastically rich and fantastically mean. Do you know the lovely Kipling story about his knighting the craftsman not for having done beautiful work but for having saved him the cost of some scroll-work?"

"With a rusty sword from behind the arras. You must be one of the few women who know their Kipling."

"Oh, I'm a very remarkable woman in many ways. So you are no nearer finding out about Richard's personality than you were?"

"No. I'm as completely bewildered as Sir Cuthbert Oliphant, bless his heart. The only difference between us is that I know I'm bewildered and he doesn't seem to be aware of it."

"Have you seen much of my woolly lamb?"

"I've seen nothing of him since his first visit, and that's three days ago. I'm beginning to wonder whether he has repented of his promise."

"Oh, no. I'm sure not. Faithfulness is his banner and creed."

"Like Richard."

"Richard?"

"His motto was, 'Loyaulté me lie.' Loyalty binds me."

There was a tentative tap at the door, and in answer to Grant's invitation, Brent Carradine appeared, hung around with top coat as usual.

"Oh! I seem to be butting in. I didn't know you were here, Miss Hallard. I met the Statue of Liberty in the corridor there, and she seemed to think you were alone, Mr. Grant."

Grant identified the Statue of Liberty without difficulty. Marta said that she was in the act of going, and that in any case Brent was a much more welcome visitor than she was nowadays. She would leave them in peace to pursue their search for the soul of a murderer.

When he had bowed her politely to the door Brent came back and sat himself down in the visitor's chair with exactly the same air that an Englishman wears when he sits down to his port after the women have left the table. Grant wondered if even the female-ridden American felt a subconscious relief at settling down to a stag party. In answer to Brent's inquiry as to how he was getting on with Oliphant, he said he found Sir Cuthbert admirably lucid.

"I've discovered who the Cat and the Rat were, incidentally. They were entirely respectable knights of the realm: William Catesby and Richard Ratcliffe. Catesby was Speaker of the House of Commons, and Ratcliffe was one of the Commissioners of Peace with Scotland. It's odd how the very sound of words makes a political jungle vicious. The Hog of course was Richard's badge. The White Boar. Do you frequent our English pubs?"

"Sure. They're one of the things I think you do better than us."

"You forgive us our plumbing for the sake of the beer at the Boar."

"I wouldn't go as far as to say I forgive it. I discount it, shall we say?"

"Magnanimous of you. Well, there's something else you've got to discount. That theory of yours that Richard hated his brother because of the contrast between his beauty and Richard's hunchbacked state. According to Sir Cuthbert, the hunchback is a myth. So is the withered arm. It appears that he had no visible deformity. At least none that mattered. His left shoulder was lower than his right, that was all. Did you find out who the contemporary historian is?"

"There isn't one."

"None at *all!*"

"Not in the sense that you mean it. There *were* writers who were contemporaries of Richard, but they wrote after his death. For the Tudors. Which puts them out of court. There is a monkish chronicle in Latin somewhere that is contemporary, but I haven't been able to get hold of it yet. One thing I have discovered though: that account of Richard III is called Sir Thomas More's not because he wrote it but because the manuscript was found among his papers. It was an unfinished copy of an account that appears elsewhere in finished form."

"Well!" Grant considered this with interest. "You mean it was More's own manuscript copy?"

"Yes. In his own writing. Made when he was about thirty-five. In those days, before printing was general, manuscript copies of books were the usual thing."

"Yes. So, if the information came from John Morton, as it did, it is just as likely that the thing was written by Morton."

"Yes."

"Which would certainly account for the—the lack of sensibility. A climber like Morton wouldn't be at all abashed by back-stairs gossip. Do you know about Morton?"

"No."

"He was a lawyer turned churchman, and the greatest pluralist on record. He chose the Lancastrian side and stayed with it until it was clear that Edward IV was home and dried. Then he made his peace with the York side and Edward made him Bishop of Ely. And vicar of God knows how many parishes besides. But after Richard's accession he backed first the Woodvilles and then Henry Tudor and ended up with a cardinal's hat as Henry VII's Archbishop of—"

"Wait a minute!" said the boy, amused. "Of *course* I know Morton. He was Morton of 'Morton's Fork.' 'You can't be spending much so how about something for the King; you're spending such a lot you must be very rich so how about something for the King.' "

"Yes. That's Morton. Henry's best thumb-screw. And I've just thought of a reason why he might have a personal hatred for Richard long before the murder of the boys."

"Yes?"

"Edward took a large bribe from Louis XI to make a dishonourable peace in France. Richard was very angry about that—it really was a disgraceful affair—and washed his hands of the business. Which included refusing a large cash offer. But Morton was very much in favour both of the deal and the cash. Indeed he took a pension from Louis. A very nice pension it was. Two thousand crowns a year. I don't suppose Richard's outspoken comments went down very well, even with good gold for a chaser."

"No. I guess not."

"And of course there would be no preferment for Morton under the straight-laced Richard as there had been under the easy-going Edward. So he would have taken the Woodville side, even if there had been no murder."

"About that murder—" the boy said; and paused.

"Yes?"

"About that murder—the murder of those two boys— isn't it odd that no one talks of it?"

"How do you mean: no one talks of it?"

"These last three days I've been going through contemporary papers; letters and what not. And no one mentions them at all."

"Perhaps they were afraid to. It was a time when it paid to be discreet."

"Yes; but I'll tell you something even odder. You know that Henry brought a Bill of Attainder against Richard, after Bosworth. Before Parliament, I mean. Well, he accuses Richard of cruelty and tyranny but doesn't even mention the murder."

"What!" said Grant, startled.

"Yes, you may well look startled."

"Are you sure!"

"Quite sure."

"But Henry got possession of the Tower immediately on his arrival in London after Bosworth. If the boys were missing it is incredible that he should not publish the fact immediately. It was the trump card in his hand." He lay in surprised silence for a little. The sparrows on the window-sill quarrelled loudly. "I can't make sense of it," he said. "What possible explanation can there be for his omission to make capital out of the fact that the boys were missing?"

Brent shifted his long legs to a more comfortable position. "There is only one explanation," he said. "And that is that the boys weren't missing."

There was a still longer silence this time, while they stared at each other.

"Oh, no, it's nonsense," Grant said. "There must be some obvious explanation that we are failing to see."

"As what, for instance?"

"I don't know. I haven't had time to think."

"I've had nearly three days to think, and I still haven't thought up a reason that will fit. *Nothing* will fit the facts except the conclusion that the boys were alive when Henry took over the Tower. It was a completely unscrupulous Act of Attainder; it accused Richard's followers—the loyal followers of an anointed King fighting against an invader—of treason. Every accusation that Henry could possibly make with any hope of getting away with it was put into the Bill. And the very worst he could accuse Richard of was the usual cruelty and tyranny. The boys aren't even mentioned."

"It's fantastic."

"It's unbelievable. But it is fact."

"What it means is that there was *no contemporary accusation at all*."

"That's about it."

"But—but wait a minute. Tyrrel was *hanged* for the murder. He actually confessed to it before he died. Wait a minute." He reached for Oliphant and sped through the pages looking for the place. "There's a full account of it here somewhere. There was no mystery about it. Even the Statue of Liberty knew about it."

"*Who?*"

"The nurse you met in the corridor. It was Tyrrel who committed the murder and he was found guilty and confessed before his death."

"Was that when Henry took over in London, then?"

"Wait a moment. Here it is." He skimmed down the paragraph. "No, it was in 1502." He realised all of a sudden what he had just said, and repeated in a new, bewildered tone: "In—1502."

"But—but—but that was—"

"Yes. Nearly twenty years afterwards."

Brent fumbled for his cigarette case, took it out, and then put it hastily away again.

"Smoke if you like," Grant said. "It's a good stiff drink I need. I don't think my brain can be working very well. I feel the way I used to feel as a child when I was blindfolded and whirled round before beginning a blindman's-buff game."

81

"Yes," said Carradine. He took out a cigarette and lighted it. "Completely in the dark, and more than a little dizzy."

He sat staring at the sparrows.

"Forty million school books can't be wrong," Grant said after a little.

"Can't they?"

"Well, can they!"

"I used to think so, but I'm not so sure nowadays."

"Aren't you being a little sudden in your scepticism?"

"Oh, it wasn't this that shook me."

"What then?"

"A little affair called the Boston Massacre. Ever heard of it?"

"Of course."

"Well, I discovered quite by accident, when I was looking up something at college, that the Boston Massacre consisted of a mob throwing stones at a sentry. The total casualties were four. I was brought up on the Boston Massacre, Mr. Grant. My twenty-eight inch chest used to swell at the very memory of it. My good red spinach-laden blood used to seethe at the thought of helpless civilians mowed down by the fire of British troops. You can't imagine what a shock it was to find that all it added up to in actual fact was a brawl that wouldn't get more than local reporting in a clash between police and strikers in any American lock-out."

As Grant made no reply to this, he squinted his eyes against the light to see how Grant was taking it. But Grant was staring at the ceiling as if he were watching patterns forming there.

"That's partly why I like research so much," Carradine volunteered; and settled back to staring at the sparrows.

Presently Grant put his hand out, wordlessly, and Carradine gave him a cigarette and lighted it for him.

They smoked in silence.

It was Grant who interrupted the sparrows' performance.

"Tonypandy," he said.

"How's that?"

But Grant was still far away.

"After all, I've seen the thing at work in my own day, haven't I?" he said, not to Carradine but to the ceiling. "It's Tonypandy."

"And what in heck is Tonypandy?" Brent asked. "It sounds like a patent medicine. Does your child get out of sorts? Does the little face get flushed, the temper short, and the limbs easily tried? Give the little one Tonypandy, and see the radiant results." And then, as Grant made no answer: "All right, then; keep your Tonypandy. I wouldn't have it as a gift."

"Tonypandy," Grant said, still in that sleep-walking voice, "is a place in the South of Wales."

"I knew it was some kind of physic."

"If you go to South Wales you will hear that, in 1910, the Government used troops to shoot down Welsh miners who were striking for their rights. You'll probably hear that Winston Churchill, who was Home Secretary at the time, was responsible. South Wales, you will be told, will never forget Tonypandy!"

Carradine had dropped his flippant air.

"And it wasn't a bit like that?"

"The actual facts are these. The rougher section of the Rhondda valley crowd had got quite out of hand. Shops were being looted and property destroyed. The Chief Constable of Glamorgan sent a request to the House Office for troops to protect the lieges. If a Chief Constable thinks a situation serious enough to ask for the help of the military a Home Secretary has very little choice in the matter. But Churchill was so horrified at the possibility of the troops coming face to face with a crowd of rioters and having to fire on them, that he stopped the movement of the troops and sent instead a body of plain, solid Metropolitan Police, armed with nothing but their rolled-up mackintoshes. The troops were kept in reserve, and all contact with the rioters was made by unarmed London police. The only bloodshed in the whole affair was a bloody nose or two. The Home Secretary was severely criticised in the House of Commons incidentally for his 'unprecedented intervention.' That was Tonypandy. That is the shooting down by troops that Wales will never forget."

"Yes," Carradine said, considering. "Yes. It's almost a parallel to the Boston affair. Someone blowing up a simple affair to huge proportions for a political end."

"The point is not that it is a parallel. The point is that *every single man* who was there knows that the story is nonsense, and yet it has never been contradicted. It will never be overtaken now. It is a completely untrue story grown to legend while the men who knew it to be untrue looked on and said nothing."

"Yes. That's very interesting; very. History as it is made."

"Yes. History."

"Give me research. After all, the truth of anything at all doesn't lie in someone's account of it. It lies in all the small facts of the time. An advertisement in a paper. The sale of a house. The price of a ring."

Grant went on looking at the ceiling, and the sparrows' clamour came back into the room.

"What amuses you?" Grant said, turning his head at last and catching the expression on his visitor's face.

"This is the first time I've seen you look like a policeman."

"I'm feeling like a policeman. I'm *thinking* like a policeman. I'm asking myself the question that every policeman asks in every case of murder: Who benefits? And for the first time it occurs to me that the glib theory that Richard got rid of the boys to make himself safer on the throne is so much nonsense. Supposing he had got rid of the boys. There were still the boys' five sisters between him and the throne. To say nothing of George's two: the boy and girl. George's son and daughter were barred by their father's attainder; but I take it that an attainder can be reversed, or annulled, or something. If Richard's claim was shaky, all those lives stood between him and safety."

"And did they all survive him?"

"I don't know. But I shall make it my business to find out. The boys' eldest sister certainly did because she became Queen of England as Henry's wife."

"Look, Mr. Grant, let's you and I start at the very beginning of this thing. Without history books, or modern versions, or anyone's opinion about anything. Truth isn't in accounts but in account books."

"A neat phrase," Grant said, complimentary. "Does it mean anything?"

"It means everything. The real history is written in forms not meant as history. In Wardrobe accounts, in Privy Purse expenses, in personal letters, in estate books. If someone, say, insists that Lady Whoosit never had a child, and you find in the account book the entry: "For the son born to my lady on Michaelmas eve: five yards of blue ribbon, fourpence halfpenny' it's a reasonably fair deduction that my lady had a son on Michaelmas eve."

"Yes. I see. All right, where do we begin."

"You're the investigator. I'm only the looker-upper."

"Research Worker."

"Thanks. What do you want to know?"

"Well, for a start, it would be useful, not to say enlightening, to know how the principals in the case reacted to Edward's death, Edward IV. I mean, Edward died unexpectedly, and his death must have caught everyone on the hop. I'd like to know how the people concerned reacted."

"That's straightforward and easy. I take it you mean what they did and not what they thought."

"Yes, of course."

"Only historians tell you what they thought. Research workers stick to what they did."

"What they did is all I want to know. I've always been a believer in the old saw that actions speak louder than words."

"Incidentally, what does the sainted Sir Thomas say that Richard did when he heard that his brother was dead?" Brent wanted to know.

"The sainted Sir Thomas (alias John Morton) says that Richard got busy being charming to the Queen and persuading her not to send a large bodyguard to escort the boy prince from Ludlow; meanwhile cooking up a plot to kidnap the boy on his way to London."

"According to the sainted More, then, Richard meant from the very first to supplant the boy."

"Oh, yes."

"Well, we shall find out, at least, who was where and doing what, whether we can deduce their intentions or not."

"That's what I want. Exactly."

"Policeman," jibed the boy. " 'Where were you at five P.M. on the night of the fifteenth inst?' "

"It works," Grant assured him. "It works."

"Well, I'll go away and work too. I'll be in again as soon as I have got the information you want. I'm very grateful to you, Mr. Grant. This is a lot better than the Peasants."

He floated away into the gathering dusk of the winter afternoon, his train-like coat giving an academic sweep and dignity to his thin young figure.

Grant switched on his lamp, and examined the pattern it made on the ceiling as if he had never seen it before.

It was a unique and engaging problem that the boy had dropped so casually into his lap. As unexpected as it was baffling.

What possible reason could there be for that lack of contemporary accusation?

Henry had not even needed proof that Richard was himself responsible. The boys were in Richard's care. If they were not to be found when the Tower was taken over, then that was far finer, thicker mud to throw at his dead rival than the routine accusations of cruelty and tyranny.

Grant ate his supper without for one moment being conscious either of its taste or its nature.

It was only when The Amazon, taking away his tray, said kindly: "Come now, that's a very good sign. Both rissoles all eaten up to the last crumb!" that he became aware that he had partaken of a meal.

For another hour he watched the lamp-pattern on the ceiling, going over the thing in his mind; going round and round it looking for some small crack that might indicate a way into the heart of the matter.

In the end he withdrew his attention altogether from the problem. Which was his habit when a conundrum proved too round and smooth and solid for immediate solution. If he slept on the proposition it might, tomorrow, show a facet that he had missed.

He looked for something that might stop his mind from

harking back to that Act of Attainder, and saw the pile of letters waiting to be acknowledged. Kind, well-wishing letters from all sorts of people; including a few old lags. The really likable old lags were an out-moded type, growing fewer and fewer daily. Their place had been taken by brash young thugs with not a spark of humanity in their egocentric souls, as illiterate as puppies and as pitiless as a circular saw. The old professional burglar was apt to be as individual as the member of any other profession, and as little vicious. Quiet little domestic men, interested in family holidays and the children's tonsils; or odd bachelors devoted to cage-birds, or second-hand bookshops, or complicated and infallible betting systems. Old-fashioned types.

No modern thug would write to say that he was sorry that a "busy" was laid aside. No such idea would ever cross a modern thug's mind.

Writing a letter when lying on one's back is a laborious business, and Grant shied away from it. But the top envelope on the pile bore the writing of his cousin Laura, and Laura would become anxious if she had no answer at all from him. Laura and he had shared summer holidays as children, and had been a little in love with each other all through one Highland summer, and that made a bond between them that had never been broken. He had better send Laura a note to say that he was alive.

He read her letter again, smiling a little; and the waters of the Turlie sounded in his ears and slid under his eyes, and he could smell the sweet cold smell of a Highland moor in winter, and he forgot for a little that he was a hospital patient and that life was sordid and boring and claustrophobic.

Pat sends what would be his love if he were a little older or just a little younger. Being nine, he says: "Tell Alan I was asking for him," and has a fly of his own invention waiting to be presented to you when you come on sick-leave. He is a little in disgrace at the moment in school, having learned for the first time that the Scots sold Charles the First to the English and having decided that he can no longer belong to such a nation. He is therefore, I understand, conducting a one-man protest strike against all things Scottish, and will learn no history, sing no song, nor memorise any geography pertaining to so deplorable a country. He announced going to bed last night that he has decided to apply for Norwegian citizenship.

Grant took his letter pad from the table and wrote in pencil:

Dearest Laura,

Would you be unbearably surprised to learn that the Princes in the Tower survived Richard III?

As ever
Alan.

P.S. I am nearly well again.

CHAPTER NINE

Do you know that the Bill attainting Richard III before Parliament didn't mention the murder of the Princes in the tower?" Grant asked the surgeon next morning.

"Really?" said the surgeon. "That's odd, isn't it?"

"Extremely odd. Can you think of an explanation?"

"Probably trying to minimise the scandal. For the sake of the family."

"He wasn't succeeded by one of his family. He was the last of his line. His successor was the first Tudor. Henry VII."

"Yes, of course. I'd forgotten. I was never any good at history. I used to use the history period to do my home algebra. They don't manage to make history very interesting in schools. Perhaps more portraits might help." He glanced up at the Richard portrait and went back to his professional inspection. "That is looking very nice and healthy, I'm glad to say. No pain to speak of now?"

And he went away, kindly and casual. He was interested in faces because they were part of his trade, but history was just something that he used for other purposes; something that he set aside in favour of algebra under the desk. He had living bodies in his care, and the future in his hands; he had no thought to spare for problems academic.

Matron, too, had more immediate worries. She listened politely while he put his difficulty to her, but he had the impression that she might say: "I should see the almoner about it if I were you." It was not her affair. She looked down from her regal eminence at the great hive below her buzzing with activity, all of it urgent and important; she

89

could hardly be expected to focus her gaze on something more than four hundred years away.

He wanted to say: "But you of all people should be interested in what can happen to royalty; in the frailness of your reputation's worth. Tomorrow a whisper may destroy you." But he was already guiltily conscious that to hinder a Matron with irrelevances was to lengthen her already lengthy morning round without reason or excuse.

The Midget did not know what an Attainder was, and made it clear that she did not care.

"It's becoming an obsession with you, that thing," she said, leaning her head at the portrait. "It's not healthy. Why don't you read some of those nice books?"

Even Marta, to whose visit he had looked forward so that he could put this odd, new proposition to her and see her reaction, even Marta was too full of wrath with Madeleine March to pay any attention to him.

"After practically promising me that she would write it! After all our get-together and my plans for when this endless thing finally comes to an end. I had even talked to Jacques about clothes! And now she decides that she must write one of her awful little detective stories. She says she must write it while it is fresh—whatever that is."

He listened to Marta's grieving with sympathy—good plays were the scarcest commodity in the world and good playwrights worth their weight in platinum—but it was like watching something through a window. The fifteenth century was more actual to him this morning than any ongoings in Shaftesbury Avenue.

"I don't suppose it will take her long to write her detective book," he said comfortingly.

"Oh, no. She does them in six weeks or so. But now that she's off the chain how do I know that I'll ever get her on again? Tony Savilla wants her to write a Marlborough play for him, and you know what Tony is when he sets his heart on something. He'd talk the pigeons off the Admiralty Arch."

She came back to the Attainder problem, briefly, before she took her leave.

"There's sure to be some explanation, my dear," she said from the door.

Of *course* there's an explanation, he wanted to shout after her, but what is it? The thing is against all likelihood and sense. Historians say that the murder caused a great revulsion of feeling against Richard, that he was hated for the crime by the common people of England, and that was why they welcomed a stranger in his place. And yet when the tale of his wrongdoing is placed before Parliament there is no mention of the crime.

Richard was dead when that complaint was drawn up, and his followers in flight or exile; his enemies were free to bring against him any charge they could think of. And they *had not thought of that spectacular murder.*

Why?

The country was reputedly ringing with the scandal of the boys' disappearance. The very recent scandal. And when his enemies collected his alleged offences against morality and the State they had not included Richard's most spectacular piece of infamy.

Why?

Henry needed every small featherweight of advantage in the precarious newness of his accession. He was unknown to the country at large and he had no right by blood to be where he was. But he hadn't used the overwhelming advantage that Richard's published crime would have given him.

Why?

He was succeeding a man of great reputation, known personally to the people from the Marches of Wales to the Scots border, a man universally liked and admired until the disappearance of his nephews. And yet he omitted to use the one real advantage he had against Richard, the unforgivable, the abhorred thing.

Why?

Only The Amazon seemed concerned about the oddity that was engaging his mind; and she not out of any feeling for Richard but because her conscientious soul was distressed at any possibility of mistake. The Amazon would go all the way down the corridor and back again to tear off a page in a loose-leaf calendar that someone had forgotten to remove. But her instinct to be worried was less strong than her instinct to comfort.

"You don't need to worry about it," she said, soothing. "There'll be some quite simple explanation that you haven't thought of. It'll come to you sometime when you're thinking of something else altogether. That's usually how I remember where something I've mislaid is. I'll be putting the kettle on in the pantry, or counting the sterile dressings as Sister doles them out, and suddenly I'll think: 'Goodness, I left it in my burberry pocket.' Whatever the thing was, I mean. So you don't have to worry about it."

Sergeant Williams was in the wilds of Essex helping the local constabulary to decide who had hit an old shopkeeper over the head with a brass scale-weight and left her dead among the shoelaces and liquorice all-sorts, so there was no help from the Yard.

There was no help from anyone until young Carradine turned up again three days later. Grant thought that his normal insouciance had a deeper tinge than usual; there was almost an air of self-congratulation about him. Being a well-brought-up child he inquired politely about Grant's physical progress, and having been reassured on that point he pulled some notes out of the capacious pocket of his coat and beamed through his horn-rims at his colleague.

"I wouldn't have the sainted More as a present," he observed pleasantly.

"You're not being offered him. There are no takers."

"He's way off the beam. Way off."

"I suspected as much. Let us have the facts. Can you begin on the day Edward died?"

"Sure. Edward died on April the 9th 1483. In London. I mean, in Westminster; which wasn't the same thing then. The Queen and the daughters were living there, *and* the younger boy. I think. The young Prince was doing lessons at Ludlow Castle in charge of the Queen's brother, Lord Rivers. The Queen's relations are very much to the fore, did you know? The place is just lousy with Woodvilles."

"Yes, I know. Go on. Where was Richard?"

"On the Scottish border."

"What!"

"Yes, I said: on the Scottish border. Caught away off base. But does he yell for a horse and go posting off to London? He does not."

"What did he do?"

"He arranged for a requiem mass at York, to which all

92

the nobility of the North were summoned, and in his presence they took an oath of loyalty to the young Prince."

"Interesting," Grant said dryly. "What did Rivers do? The Queen's brother?"

"On the 24th of April he set out with the Prince for London. With two thousand men and a large supply of arms."

"What did he want the arms for?"

"Don't ask me. I'm only a research worker. Dorset, the elder of the Queen's two sons by her first marriage, took over both the arsenal and the treasure in the Tower and began to fit up ships to command the Channel. And Council orders were issued *in the name of Rivers and Dorset*—'avunculus Regis' and 'frater Regis uterinus' respectively—with no mention of Richard. Which was decidedly off-colour when you remember—if you ever knew—that in his will Edward had appointed Richard guardian of the boy and Protector of the Kingdom in case of any minority. Richard alone, mind you, without a colleague."

"Yes, that is in character, at least. He must always have had complete faith in Richard. Both as a person and as an administrator. Did Richard come south with a young army too?"

"No. He came with six hundred gentlemen of the North, all in deep mourning. He arrived at Northampton on April the 29th. He had apparently expected to join up with the Ludlow crowd there; but that is report and you have only a historian's word for it. But the Ludlow procession—Rivers and the young Prince—had gone on to Stoney Stratford without waiting for him. The person who actually met him at Northampton was the Duke of Buckingham with three hundred men. Do you know Buckingham?"

"We have a nodding acquaintance. He was a friend of Edward's."

"Yes. He arrived post haste from London."

"With the news of what was going on."

"It's a fair deduction. He wouldn't bring three hundred men just to express his condolences. Anyhow a Council was held there and then—he had all the human material
93

for a proper Council in his own train and Buckingham's, and Rivers and his three aides were arrested and sent to the North, while Richard went on with the young Prince to London. They arrived in London on the 4th of May."

"Well, that is very nice and clear. And what is clearest of all is that, considering time and distances, the sainted More's account of his writing sweet letters to the Queen to induce her to send only a small escort for the boy, is nonsense."

"Bunk."

"Indeed, Richard did just what one would expect him to do. He must of course have known the provisions of Edward's will. What his actions suggest is just what one would expect them to suggest; his own sorrow and his care for the boy. A requiem mass and an oath of allegiance."

"Yes."

"Where does the break in this orthodox pattern come? I mean: in Richard's behaviour."

"Oh, not for a long time. When he arrived in London he found that the Queen, the younger boy, the daughters, and her first-marriage son, Dorset, had all bolted into sanctuary at Westminster. But apart from that things seem to have been normal."

"Did he take the boy to the Tower?"

Carradine riffled through his notes. "I don't remember. Perhaps I didn't get that. I was only—Oh, yes, here it is. No, he took the boy to the Bishop's Palace in St. Paul's Churchyard, and he himself went to stay with his mother at Baynard's Castle. Do you know where that was? I don't."

"Yes. It was the York's town house. It stood on the bank of the river just a little way west of St. Paul's."

"Oh. Well, he stayed there until June the 5th, when his wife arrived from the North and they went to stay in a house called Crosby Place."

"It is still called Crosby Place. It has been moved to Chelsea, and the window Richard put into it may not still be there—I haven't seen it lately—but the building is there."

"It is?" Carradine said, delighted. "I'll go and see it right away. It's a very domestic tale when you think of it, isn't it? Staying with his mother until his wife gets to town,

94

and then moving in with her. Was Crosby Place theirs, then?"

"Richard had leased it, I think. It belonged to one of the Aldermen of London. So there is no suggestion of opposition to his Protectorship, or of change of plans, when he arrived in London."

"Oh, no. He was acknowledged Protector before he ever arrived in London."

"How do you know that?"

"In the Patent Rolls he is called Protector on two occasions—let me see—April 21st (that's less than a fortnight after Edward's death) and May the 2nd (that's two days before he arrived in London at all)."

"All right; I'm sold. And no fuss? No hint of trouble?"

"Not that I can find. On the 5th of June he gave detailed orders for the boy's coronation on the 22nd. He even had letters of summons sent out to the forty squires who would be made knights of the Bath. It seems it was the custom for the King to knight them on the occasion of his coronation."

"The 5th," Grant said musingly. "And he fixed the coronation for the 22nd. He wasn't leaving himself much time for a switch-over."

"No. There's even a record of the order for the boy's coronation clothes."

"And then what?"

"Well," Carradine said, apologetic, "that's as far as I've got. Something happened at a Council—on the 8th of June, I think—but the contemporary account is in the *Mémoires* of Philippe de Comines and I haven't been able to get hold of a copy so far. But someone has promised to let me see a copy of Mandrot's 1901 printing of it tomorrow. It seems that the Bishop of Bath broke some news to the Council on June the 8th. Do you know the Bishop of Bath? His name was Stillington."

"Never heard of him."

"He was a Fellow of All Souls, whatever that is, and a Canon of York, whatever *that* may be."

"Both learned and respectable, it appears."

"Well, we'll see."

"Have you turned up any contemporary historians—other than Comines?"

"Not any, so far, who wrote before Richard's death. Comines has a French bias but not a Tudor one, so he's more trustworthy than an Englishman writing about Richard under the Tudors would be. But I've got a lovely sample for you of how history is made. I found it when I was looking up the contemporary writers. You know that one of the things they tell about Richard III is that he killed Henry VI's only son in cold blood after the battle of Tewkesbury? Well, believe it or not, that story is made up out of whole cloth. You can trace it from the very time it was first told. It's the perfect answer to people who say there's no smoke without fire. Believe me, this smoke was made by rubbing two pieces of dry stick together."

"But Richard was just a boy at the time of Tewkesbury."

"He was eighteen, I think. And a very bonny fighter by all contemporary accounts. They were the same age, Henry's son and Richard. Well, *all* the contemporary accounts, of whatever complexion, are unanimous in saying that he was killed during the battle. Then the fun begins."

Carradine fluttered through his notes impatiently.

"Goldarn it, what did I do with it? Ah. Here we are. Now. Fabyan, writing for Henry VII, says that the boy was captured and brought before Edward IV, was struck in the face by Edward with his gauntlet and immediately slain by the King's servants. Nice? But Polydore Virgil goes one better. He says that the murder was done in person by George, Duke of Clarence, Richard, Duke of Gloucester, and William, Lord Hastings. Hall adds Dorset to the murderers. But that didn't satisfy Holinshed: Holinshed reports that it was Richard, Duke of Gloucester who struck the first blow. How do you like that? Best quality Tonypandy, isn't it?"

"Pure Tonypandy. A dramatic story with not a word of truth in it. If you can bear to listen to a few sentences of the sainted More. I'll give you another sample of how history is made."

"The sainted More makes me sick at the stomach but I'll listen."

Grant looked for the paragraph he wanted, and read:

Some wise men also ween that his drift [that is,

Richard's drift] covertly conveyed, lacked not in helping forth his brother Clarence to his death; which he resisted openly, howbeit somewhat, as men deemed, more faintly than he that were heartily minded to his weal. And they who deem thus think that he, long time in King Edward's life, forethought to be King in case that the King his brother (whose life he looked that evil diet should shorten) should happen to decrease (as indeed he did) while his children were young. And they deem that for this intent he was glad of his brother Clarence's death, whose life must needs have hindered him so intending whether the same Clarence had kept true to his nephew the young King or enterprised to be King himself. But of all this point there is no certainty, and whoso divineth upon conjectures may as well shoot too far as too short.

"The mean, burbling, insinuating old bastard," said Carradine sweetly.

"Were you clever enough to pick out the one positive statement in all that speculation?"

"Oh, yes."

"You spotted it? That was smart of you. I had to read it three times before I got the one unqualified fact."

"That Richard protested openly against his brother George being put to death."

"Yes."

"Of course, with all that 'men say' stuff," Carradine observed, "the impression that is left is just the opposite. I told you. I wouldn't have the sainted More as a present."

"I think we ought to remember that it is John Morton's account and not the sainted More's."

"The sainted More sounds better. Besides, he liked the thing well enough to be copying it out."

Grant, the one-time soldier, lay thinking of the expert handling of that very sticky situation at Northampton.

"It was neat of him to mop up Rivers' two thousand without any open clash."

"I expect they preferred the King's brother to the Queen's brother, if they were faced with it."

"Yes. And of course a fighting man has a better chance with troops than a man who writes books."

"Did Rivers write books?"

"He wrote the first book printed in England. Very cultured, he was."

"Huh. It doesn't seem to have taught him not to try conclusions with a man who was a brigadier at eighteen and general before he was twenty-five. That's one thing that has surprised me, you know."

"Richard's qualities as a soldier?"

"No, his youth. I'd always thought of him as a middle-aged grouch. He was only thirty-two when he was killed at Bosworth."

"Tell me: when Richard took over the boy's guardianship, at Stoney Stratford, did he make a clean sweep of the Ludlow crowd? I mean, was the boy separated from all the people he had been growing up with?"

"Oh, no. His tutor, Dr. Alcock, came on to London with him, for one."

"So there was no panic clearing-out of everyone who might be on the Woodville side; everyone who might influence the boy against him."

"Seems not. Just the four arrests."

"Yes. A very neat, discriminating operation altogether. I felicitate Richard Plantagenet."

"I'm positively beginning to like the guy. Well, I'm going along now to look at Crosby Place. I'm tickled pink at the thought of actually looking at a place he lived in. And tomorrow I'll have that copy of Comines, and let you know what he says about events in England in 1483, and what Robert Stillington, Bishop of Bath, told the Council in June of that year."

CHAPTER TEN

What Stillington told the Council on that summer day in 1483 was, Grant learned, that he had married Edward IV to Lady Eleanor Butler, a daughter of the first Earl of Shrewsbury, before Edward married Elizabeth Woodville.

"Why had he kept it to himself so long?" he asked when he had digested the news.

"Edward had commanded him to keep it secret. Naturally."

"Edward seems to have made a habit of secret marriages," Grant said dryly.

"Well, it must have been difficult for him, you know, when he came up against unassailable virtue. There was nothing for it but marriage. And he was so used to getting his own way with women—what with his looks and his crown—that he couldn't have taken very resignedly to frustration."

"Yes. That was the pattern of the Woodville marriage. The indestructibly virtuous beauty with the gilt hair, and the secret wedding. So Edward had used the same formula on a previous occasion, if Stillington's story was true. Was it true?"

"Well, in Edward's time, it seems, he was in turn both Privy Seal and Lord Chancellor, and he had been an ambassador to Brittany. So Edward either owed him something or liked him. And he, on his part, had no reason to cook up anything against Edward. Supposing he was the cooking sort."

"No, I suppose not."

"Anyway, the thing was put to Parliament so we don't have to take just Stillington's word for it."

"To Parliament!"

"Sure. Everything was open and above board. There was a very long meeting of the Lords at Westminster on the 9th. Stillington brought in his evidence and his witnesses, and a report was prepared to put before Parliament when it assembled on the 25th. On the 10th Richard sent a letter to the city of York asking for troops to protect and support him."

"Ha! Trouble at last."

"Yes. On the 11th he sent a similar letter to his cousin Lord Nevill. So the danger was real."

"It must have been real. A man who dealt so economically with that unexpected and very nasty situation at Northampton wouldn't be one to lose his head at a threat."

"On the 20th he went with a small body of retainers to the Tower—did you know that the Tower was the royal residence in London, and not a prison at all?"

"Yes, I knew that. It got its prison meaning only because nowadays being sent to the Tower has one meaning only. And of course because, being the royal castle in London, and the only strong keep, offenders were sent there for safe keeping in the days before we had His Majesty's Prisons. What did Richard go to the Tower for?"

"He went to interrupt a meeting of the conspirators, and arrested Lord Hastings, Lord Stanley, and one John Morton, Bishop of Ely."

"I thought we would arrive at John Morton sooner or later!"

"A proclamation was issued, giving details of the plot to murder Richard, but apparently no copy now exists. Only one of the conspirators was beheaded, and that one, oddly enough, seems to have been an old friend of both Edward and Richard. Lord Hastings."

"Yes, according to the sainted More he was rushed down to the courtyard and beheaded on the nearest log."

"Rushed nothing," said Carradine disgustedly. "He was beheaded a week later. There's a contemporary letter about it that gives the date. Moreover, Richard couldn't have done it out of sheer vindictiveness, because he granted Hastings' forfeited estates to his widow, and restored the children's right of succession to them—which they had automatically lost."

"No, the death of Hastings must have been inevitable," said Grant, who was thumbing through More's *Richard III*. "Even the sainted More says: 'Undoubtedly the Protector loved him well, and was loth to have lost him.' What happened to Stanley and to John Morton?"

"Stanley was pardoned—What are you groaning about?"

"Poor Richard. That was his death warrant."

"Death warrant? How could pardoning Stanley be his death warrant?"

"Because it was Stanley's sudden decision to go over to the other side that lost Richard the battle of Bosworth."

"You don't say."

"Odd to think that if Richard had seen to it that Stanley went to the block like his much-loved Hastings, he would have won the battle of Bosworth, there would never have been any Tudors, and the hunchbacked monster that appears in Tudor tradition would never have been invented. On his previous showing he would probably have had the best and most enlightened reign in history. What was done to Morton?"

"Nothing."

"Another mistake."

"Or at least nothing to signify. He was put into gentlemanly detention under the care of Buckingham. The people who did go to the block were the heads of the conspiracy that Richard had arrested at Northampton: Rivers and Co. And Jane Shore was sentenced to do penance."

"Jane Shore? What on earth has she got to do with the case? I thought she was Edward's mistress?"

"So she was. But Hastings inherited her from Edward, it seems. Or rather—let me see—Dorset did. And she was go-between between the Hastings side of the conspiracy and the Woodville side. One of Richard's letters existing today is about her. About Jane Shore."

"What about her?"

"His Solicitor-General wanted to marry her; when he was King, I mean."

"And he agreed?"

"He agreed. It's a lovely letter. More in sorrow than in anger—with a kind of twinkle in it."

" 'Lord, what fools these mortals be!' "

"That's it exactly."

"No vindictiveness there, either, it seems."

"No. Quite the opposite. You know, I know it isn't my business to think or draw deductions—I'm just the Research Worker—but it does strike me that Richard's ambition was to put an end to the York-Lancaster fight once and for all."

"What makes you think that?"

"Well, I've been looking at his coronation lists. It was the best-attended coronation on record, incidentally. You can't help being struck by the fact that practically nobody stayed away. Lancaster *or* York."

"Including the weather-cock Stanley, I suppose."

"I suppose so. I don't know them well enough to remember them individually."

"Perhaps you're right about his wanting a final end to the York-Lancaster feud. Perhaps his lenience with Stanley was due to that very thing."

"Was Stanley a Lancastrian, then?"

"No, but he was married to an abnormally rabid one. His wife was Margaret Beaufort, and the Beauforts were the reverse side, so to speak—the illegitimate side—of the Lancaster family. Not that her by-blow side worried her. *Or* her son."

"Who was her son?"

"Henry VII."

Carradine whistled, long and low.

"You actually mean to say that Lady Stanley was Henry's mother."

"She was. By her first husband Edmund Tudor."

"But—but Lady Stanley had a place of honour at Richard's coronation. She carried the Queen's train. I noticed that because I thought it quaint. Carrying the train, I mean. In our country we don't carry trains. It's an honour, I take it."

"It's a thundering great honour. Poor Richard. Poor Richard. It didn't work."

"What didn't?"

"Magnanimity." He lay thinking about it while Carradine shuffled through his notes. "So Parliament accepted the evidence of Stillington."

102

"They did more. They incorporated it into an Act, giving Richard the title to the crown. It was called Titulus Regius."

"For a holy man of God, Stillington wasn't cutting a very glorious figure. But I suppose that to have talked sooner would have been to compass his own ruin."

"You're a bit hard on him, aren't you? There wasn't any need to talk sooner. No harm was being done anyone."

"What about Lady Eleanor Butler?"

"She died in a convent. She's buried in the Church of the White Carmelites at Norwich, in case you're interested. As long as Edward was alive no wrong was being done anyone. But when it came to the question of succession, then he *had* to talk, whatever kind of figure he cut."

"Yes. Of course you're right. So the children were proclaimed illegitimate, in open Parliament. And Richard was crowned. With all the nobility of England in attendance. Was the Queen still in sanctuary?"

"Yes. But she had let the younger boy join his brother."

"When was that?"

Carradine searched through his notes. "On June the 16th. I've put: 'At the request of the Archbishop of Canterbury. Both boys living at the Tower.'"

"That was after the news had broken. The news that they were illegitimate."

"Yes." He tidied his notes into some kind of neatness and put them away in the enormous pocket. "That seems to be all, to date. But here's the pay-off." He gathered his train from either side of him on to his knees with a gesture that both Marta and King Richard might have envied. "You know that Act, that Titulus Regius."

"Yes; what about it?"

"Well, when Henry VII came to the throne he ordered that the Act should be repealed, without being read. He ordered that the the Act itself, should be destroyed, and forbade any copies to be kept. Anyone who kept a copy was to be fined and imprisoned during his pleasure."

Grant stared in great astonishment.

"*Henry VII!*" he said. "Why? What possible difference could it make to him?"

"I haven't a glimmer of an idea. But I mean to find out before I'm much older. Meanwhile, here is something to

103

keep you amused till the Statue of Liberty brings your British tea."

He dropped a paper on to Grant's chest.

"What is this?" Grant said, looking at the torn-out page of a note-book.

"It's that letter of Richard's about Jane Shore. I'll be seeing you."

Left alone by himself in the quiet, Grant turned over the page and read.

The contrast between the sprawling childish handwriting and the formal phrases of Richard's imagining was piquant in the extreme. But what neither the untidy modern script nor the dignified phrases could destroy was the flavour of the letter. The bouquet of good humour that came up from the page as a bouquet comes up from a good-humoured wine. Translated into modern terms it said:

> I hear to my great astonishment that Tom Lynom wants to marry Will Shore's wife. Apparently he is infatuated with her, and is quite determined about it. Do, my dear Bishop, send for him and see if you can talk some sense into his silly head. If you can't, and if there is no bar to their marriage from the Church's point of view, then I agree to it, but tell him to postpone the marriage till I am back in London. Meanwhile this will suffice to secure her release, on surety for her good behaviour, and I suggest that you hand her over for the time being to the care of her father, or anyone else who seems good to you.

It was certainly, as young Carradine had said, "more in sorrow than in anger." Indeed, considering that it was written about a woman who had done him a deadly wrong, its kindness and good temper were remarkable. And this was a case where no personal advantage could come to him from magnanimity. The broadmindedness that had sought for a York-Lancaster peace might not have been disinterested; it would have been enormously to his advantage to have a united country to rule. But this letter to the Bishop of Lincoln was a small private matter, and the release of Jane Shore of no importance to anyone but the infatuated Tom Lynom. Richard had nothing to gain by his generosity. His instinct to see a friend happy was apparently greater than his instinct for revenge.

Indeed, this instinct for revenge seemed to be lacking to a degree that would be surprising in any red-blooded male, and quite astonishing in the case of that reputed monster Richard III.

CHAPTER ELEVEN

The letter lasted Grant very nicely until The Amazon brought his tea. He listened to the twentieth century sparrows on his window-sill and marvelled that he should be reading phrases that formed in a man's mind more than four hundred years ago. What a fantastic idea it would have seemed to Richard that anyone would be reading that short, intimate letter about Shore's wife, and wondering about him, four hundred years afterwards.

"There's a letter for you, now isn't that nice?" The Amazon said, coming in with his two pieces of bread-and-butter and a rock bun.

Grant took his eyes from the uncompromising healthiness of the rock bun and saw that the letter was from Laura.

He opened it with pleasure.

Dear Alan [said Laura]
    Nothing (repeat: nothing) would surprise me about history. Scotland has large monuments to two women martyrs drowned for their faith, in spite of the fact that they weren't drowned at all and neither was a martyr anyway. They were convicted of treason—fifth column work for the projected invasion from Holland, I think. Anyhow on a purely civil charge. They were reprieved *on their own petition* by the Privy Council, and the reprieve is in the Privy Council Register to this day.
    This, of course, hasn't daunted the Scottish collectors of martyrs, and the tale of their sad end, complete with heart-rending dialogue, is to be found in every Scot-

tish bookcase. Entirely different dialogue in each collection. And the gravestone of one of the women, in Wigtown churchyard, reads:

> Murdered for owning Christ supreme
> Head of his Church, and no more crime
> But her not owning Prelacy
> And not abjuring Presbytry
> Within the sea tied to a stake
> She suffered for Christ Jesus sake.

They are even a subject for fine Presbyterian sermons, I understand—though on that point I speak from hearsay. And tourists come and shake their heads over the monuments with their moving inscriptions, and a very profitable time is had by all.

All this in spite of the fact that the original collector of the material, canvassing the Wigtown district only forty years after the supposed martyrdom and at the height of the Presbyterian triumph, complains that "many deny that this happened"; and couldn't find any eyewitnesses at all.

It is very good news that you are convalescent, and a great relief to us all. If you manage it well your sick leave can coincide with the spring run. The water is very low at the moment, but by the time you are better it should be deep enough to please both the fish and you.

Love from us all,
Laura.

P.S. It's an odd thing but when you tell someone the true facts of a mythical tale they are indignant not with the teller but with you. They don't *want* to have their ideas upset. It rouses some vague uneasiness in them, I think, and they resent it. So they reject it and refuse to think about it. If they were merely indifferent it would be natural and understandable. But it is much stronger than that, much more positive. They are annoyed.

Very odd, isn't it?

More Tonypandy, he thought.

He began to wonder just how much of the school book which up to now had represented British history for him was Tonypandy.

He went back, now that he knew a few facts, to read the sainted More again. To see how the relevant passages sounded now.

If, when he had read them merely by the light of his own critical mind, they had seemed to him curiously tattling, and in places absurd, they now read plain abominable. He was what Laura's small Pat was in the habit of calling "scunnered." And he was also puzzled.

This was Morton's account. Morton the eyewitness, the participant. Morton must have known with minute accuracy what took place between the beginning and end of June that year. And yet there was no mention of Lady Eleanor Butler; no mention of Titulus Regius. According to Morton, Richard's case has been that Edward was previously married to his mistress Elizabeth Lucy. But Elizabeth Lucy, Morton pointed out, had denied that she was ever married to the King.

Why did Morton set up a ninepin just to knock it down again?

Why the substitution of Elizabeth Lucy for Eleanor Butler?

Because he could deny with truth that Lucy was ever married to the King, but could not do the same in the case of Eleanor Butler?

Surely the presumption was that it was very important to someone or other that Richard's claim that the children were illegitimate should be shown to be untenable.

And since Morton—in the handwriting of the sainted More—was writing for Henry VII, then that someone was presumably Henry VII. The Henry VII who had destroyed Titulus Regius and forbidden anyone to keep a copy.

Something Carradine had said came back into Grant's mind.

Henry had caused the Act to be repealed *without being read*.

It was so important to Henry that the contents of the

Act should not be brought to mind that he had specially provided for its unquoted destruction.

Why should it be of such importance to Henry VII?

How could it matter to *Henry* what Richard's rights were? It was not as if he could say: Richard's claim was a trumped-up one, therefore mine is good. Whatever wretched small claim Henry Tudor might have was a Lancastrian one, and the heirs of York did not enter into the matter.

Then why should it have been of such paramount importance to Henry that the contents of Titulus Regius should be forgotten?

Why hide away Eleanor Butler, and bring in in her place a mistress whom no one ever suggested was married to the King?

This problem lasted Grant very happily till just before supper; when the porter came in with a note for him.

"The front hall says that young American friend of yours left this for you," the porter said, handing him a folded sheet of paper.

"Thank you," said Grant. "What do you know about Richard the Third?"

"Is there a prize?"

"What for?"

"The quiz."

"No, just the satisfaction of intellectual curiosity. What *do* you know about Richard III?"

"He was the first multiple murderer."

"Multiple? I thought it was two nephews?"

"No, oh, no. I don't know much history but I do know that. Murdered his brother, and his cousin, and the poor old King in the Tower, and then finished off with his little nephews. A wholesale performer."

Grant considered this.

"If I told you that he never murdered anyone at all, what would you say?"

"I'd say that you're perfectly entitled to your opinion. Some people believe the earth is flat. Some people believe the world is going to end in A.D. 2000. Some people believe that it began less than five thousand years ago.

You'll hear far funnier things than that at Marble Arch of a Sunday."

"So you wouldn't even entertain the idea for a moment?"

"I find it entertaining all right, but not what you might call very plausible, shall we say? But don't let me stand in your way. Try it out on a better bombing range. You take it to Marble Arch one Sunday, and I'll bet you'll find followers aplenty. Maybe start a movement."

He made a gay sketchy half-salute with his hand and went away humming to himself; secure and impervious.

So help me, Grant thought, I'm not far off it. If I get any deeper into this thing I *will* be standing on a soapbox at Marble Arch.

He unfolded the message from Carradine, and read: "You said that you wanted to know whether the other heirs to the throne survived Richard. As well as the boys, I mean. I forgot to say: would you make out a list of them for me, so that I can look them up. I think it's going to be important."

Well, if the world in general went on its humming way, brisk and uncaring, at least he had young America on his side.

He put aside the sainted More, with its Sunday-paper accounts of hysterical scenes and wild accusations, and reached for the sober student's account of history so that he might catalogue the possible rivals to Richard III in the English succession.

And as he put down More-Morton, he was reminded of something.

That hysterical scene during the Council in the Tower which was reported by More, that frantic outburst on Richard's part against the sorcery that had withered his arm, had been against Jane Shore.

The contrast between the reported scene, pointless and repellent even to a disinterested reader, and the kind, tolerant, almost casual air of the letter that Richard had actually written about her, was staggering.

So help me, he thought again, if I had to choose between the man who wrote that account and the man who wrote that letter I'd take the man who wrote the letter, whatever either of them had done besides.

The thought of Morton made him postpone his listing of the York heirs until he had found out what eventually became of John Morton. It seemed that, having used his leisure as Buckingham's guest to organise a joint Woodville-Lancastrian effort (in which Henry Tudor would bring ships and troops from France and Dorset and the rest of the Woodville tribe would meet him with what English malcontents they could induce to follow them), he escaped to his old hunting ground in the Ely district, and from there to the continent. And did not come back until he came in the wake of a Henry who had won both Bosworth and a crown; being himself on the way to Canterbury and a cardinal's hat and immortality as Morton of "Morton's Fork." Almost the only thing that any schoolboy remembered about his master Henry VII.

For the rest of the evening Grant pottered happily through the history books, collecting heirs.

There was no lack of them. Edward's five, George's boy and girl. And if these were discounted, the first through illegitimacy and the second through attainder, there was another possible: his elder sister Elizabeth's boy. Elizabeth was Duchess of Suffolk, and her son was John de la Pole, Earl of Lincoln.

There was, too, in the family, a boy whose existence Grant had not suspected. It appeared that the delicate child at Middleham was not Richard's only son. He had a love-child; a boy called John. John of Gloucester. A boy of no importance in rank but acknowledged and living in the household. It was an age when a bend sinister was accepted without grief. Indeed the Conqueror had made it fashionable. And conquerors from then on had advertised its lack of disadvantage. By way of compensation, perhaps.

EDWARD	ELIZABETH	GEORGE	RICHARD
Edward, Prince of Wales	John de la Pole, Earl of Lincoln	Edward, Earl of Warwick	John of Gloucester
Richard, Duke of York		Margaret, Countess of Salisbury	
Elizabeth			
Cicely			
Anne			
Katherine			
Bridget			

He copied it out again for young Carradine's use, wondering how it could ever have occurred to anyone, Richard most of all, that the elimination of Edward's two boys would have kept him safe from rebellion. The place was what young Carradine would call just lousy with heirs. Swarming with focuses (or was it foci?) for disaffection.

It was brought home to him for the first time not only what a useless thing the murder of the boys would have been, but what a *silly* thing.

And if there was anything that Richard of Gloucester was not, beyond a shadow of a shadow of doubt, it was silly.

He looked up Oliphant to see what Oliphant had to say on this obvious crack in the story.

"It is strange," said Oliphant, "that Richard does not seem to have published any version of their deaths."

It was more than strange: it was incomprehensible.

If Richard had wanted to murder his brother's sons then he most certainly would have done it expertly. They would have died of a fever, and their bodies would have been exposed to the public gaze as royal bodies habitually were, so that all men would know that they were in fact departed from this life.

No one can say that a man is incapable of murder—after long years on the Embankment Grant knew that only too well—but one can be sure to within one degree of the absolute when a man is incapable of silliness.

Oliphant had no doubts about the murder, nevertheless.

Richard, according to Oliphant, was Richard the Monster. Perhaps when an historian was covering a field as large as the Middle Ages and the Renaissance he had no time to stop and analyse detail. Oliphant accepted the sainted More, even while he paused in flight to wonder at an oddity here and there. Not seeing that the oddities ate away at the very foundations of his theory.

Having Oliphant in his hand, he went on with Oliphant. On through the triumphal progress through England after the coronation. Oxford, Gloucester, Worcester, Warwick. No dissentient voice was recorded on that tour. Only a chorus of blessing and thanksgiving. A rejoicing that good government was to be the order of the day for a lifetime to come. That, after all, Edward's sudden death had not condemned them to years of faction and a new civil struggle over the person of his son.

And yet it was during this triumph, this unanimous acclamation, this universal hosanna, that (according to Oliphant, riding in the pocket of the sainted More) Richard sent Tyrrel back to London to make away with the boys who were doing lessons in the Tower. Between July 7th and 15th. At Warwick. In the very summer of his safety, in the heart of the York country on the borders of Wales, he planned the destruction of two discredited children.

It was a highly unlikely story.

He began to wonder whether historians were possessed of minds any more commonsensical than those Great Minds he had encountered, who had been so credulous.

He must find out without delay why, if Tyrrel did that job in 1485, he wasn't brought to book until twenty years afterwards. Where had he been in the meantime?

But Richard's summer was like an April day. Full of a promise that came to nothing. In the autumn he had to face that Woodville-Lancastrian invasion which Morton had cooked up before leaving these shores himself. The Lancastrian part of the affair did Morton proud: they came with a fleet of French ships and a French army. But the Woodville side could provide nothing better than sporadic little gatherings in widely separated centres: Guildford, Salisbury, Maidstone, Newbury, Exeter, and Brecon. The English wanted no part of Henry Tudor, whom they knew only too well. Even the English weather would have none of them. And Dorset's hope of seeing his half-sister Elizabeth queen of England as Henry Tudor's wife was washed away in Severn floods. Henry tried to land in the West, but found Devon and Cornwall up in indignant arms at the idea. He therefore sailed away to France again, to wait for a luckier day. And Dorset went to join in the growing crowd of Woodville exiles hanging round the French court.

So Morton's plan was washed away in autumn rain and English indifference, and Richard could be at peace for a little; but with the spring came a grief that nothing could wash away. The death of his son.

"The King is said to have shown signs of desperate grief; he was not such an unnatural monster as to be destitute of the feeling of a father," said the historian.

Nor of a husband, it seemed. The same marks of suffering were reported of him less than a year later, when Anne died.

And after that there was nothing but the waiting for the renewal of the invasion that had failed; the keeping of England in a state of defence, and the anxiety that that drain on the Exchequer brought him.

He had done what good he could. He had given his name to a model Parliament. He had made peace at last with Scotland and arranged a marriage between his niece and James III's son. He had tried very hard for a peace with France, but had failed. At the French court was Henry Tudor, and Henry Tudor was France's white-headed boy. It would be only a matter of time before Henry landed in England, this time with better backing.

Grant suddenly remembered Lady Stanley, that ardent Lancastrian mother of Henry. What part had Lady Stanley had in that autumn invasion that had put paid to Richard's summer?

He hunted through the solid print until he found it.

Lady Stanley had been found guilty of treasonable correspondence with her son.

But again Richard had proved too lenient for his own good, it seemed. Her estates were forfeit, but they were handed over to her husband. And so was Lady Stanley. For safe keeping. The bitter joke being that Stanley had almost certainly been as knowledgeable about the invasion as his wife.

Truly, the monster was not running according to form.

As Grant was falling asleep a voice said in his mind: "If the boys were murdered in July, and the Woodville-Lancastrian invasion took place in October, why didn't they use the murder of the children as a rallying call?"

The invasion had, of course, been planned before there was any question of murder; it was a full-dress affair of fifteen ships and five thousand mercenaries and must have taken a long time to prepare. But by the time of the rising the rumours of Richard's infamy must have been widespread if there were any rumours at all. Why had they not gone shouting his crime through England, so that the horror of it brought men flocking to their cause?

CHAPTER TWELVE

"Cool off, cool off," he said to himself when he woke next morning, "you're beginning to be partisan. That's no way to conduct an investigation."

So, by way of moral discipline, he became prosecutor.

Supposing that the Butler story was a frame-up. A story concocted with Stillington's help. Supposing that both Lords and Commons were willing to be hoodwinked in the hope of stable Government to come.

Did that bring one any nearer the murder of the two boys?

It didn't, did it?

If the story was false, the person to be got rid of was Stillington. Lady Eleanor had died in her convent long ago, so was not there to blow Titulus Regius to pieces any time she had a mind. But Stillington could. And Stillington evidently showed no difficulty in going on living. He survived the man he had put on the throne.

The sudden jar in the proceedings, the abrupt break in the pattern of the coronation preparation, was either wonderful stage-managing or just what one would expect if the thunderclap of Stillington's confession descended on unprepared ears. Richard was—what? Eleven? Twelve?—when the Butler contract was signed and witnessed; it was unlikely that he knew anything of it.

If the Butler story was an invention to oblige Richard, then Richard must have rewarded Stillington. But there was no sign of Stillington's being obliged with a cardinal's hat, or preferment, or office.

But the surest evidence that the Butler story was true lay in Henry VII's urgent need to destroy it. If it were false, then all he had to do to discredit Richard was to bring it into the open and make Stillington eat his words. Instead he hushed it up.

At this point Grant realised with disgust that he was back on the Defence side again. He decided to give it up. He would take to Lavinia Fitch, or Rupert Rouge, or some other of the fashionable authors lying in such expensive neglect on his table, and forget Richard Plantagenet until such time as young Carradine appeared to renew the inquisition.

He put the family-tree sketch of Cicely Nevill's grandchildren into an envelope and addressed it to Carradine, and gave it to The Midget to post. Then he turned down the portrait that was leaning against the books, so that he should not be seduced by that face which Sergeant Williams had placed, without hesitation, on the bench, and reached for Silas Weekley's *The Sweat and the Furrow.* Thereafter he went from Silas's seamy wrestlings to Lavinia's tea-cups, and from Lavinia's tea-cups to Rupert's cavortings in the *coulisses,* with a growing dissatisfaction, until Brent Carradine once more turned up in his life.

Carradine regarded him anxiously and said: "You don't look so bright as last time I saw you, Mr. Grant. You not doing so well?"

"Not where Richard is concerned, I'm not," Grant said. "But I've got a new piece of Tonypandy for you."

And he handed him Laura's letter about the drowned women who were never drowned.

Carradine read it with a delight that grew on him like slow sunlight coming out, until eventually he glowed.

"My, but that's wonderful. That's very superior, first growth, dyed-in-the-wool Tonypandy, isn't it? Lovely, lovely. You didn't know about this before? And you a Scotsman?"

"I'm only a Scot once removed," Grant pointed out. "No; I knew that none of these Covenanters died 'for their Faith,' of course; but I didn't know that one of them—or rather, two of them—hadn't died at all."

"They didn't die for their Faith?" Carradine repeated, bewildered. "D'you mean that the *whole thing's* Tonypandy?"

117

Grant laughed. "I suppose it is," he said, surprised. "I never thought about it before. I've known so long that the 'martyrs' were no more martyrs than that thug who is going to his death for killing that old shop-keeper in Essex, that I've ceased to think about it. No one in Scotland went to his death for anything but civil crime."

"But I thought they were very holy people—the Covenanters, I mean."

"You've been looking at nineteenth-century pictures of conventicles. The reverent little gathering in the heather listening to the preacher; young rapt faces, and white hair blowing in the winds of God. The Covenanters were the exact equivalent of the I.R.A. in Ireland. A small irreconcilable minority, and as bloodthirsty a crowd as ever disgraced a Christian nation. If you went to church on Sunday instead of to a conventicle, you were liable to wake on Monday and find your barn burned or your horses ham-strung. If you were more open in your disapproval you were shot. The men who shot Archbishop Sharp in his daughter's presence, in broad daylight on a road in Fife, were the heroes of the movement. 'Men of courage and zeal for the cause of God,' according to their admiring followers. They lived safe and swaggering among their Covenanting fans in the West for years. It was a 'preacher of the gospel' who shot Bishop Honeyman in an Edinburgh street. And they shot the old parish priest of Carsphairn on his own doorstep."

"It does sound like Ireland, doesn't it?" Carradine said.

"They were actually worse than the I.R.A. because there was a fifth column element in it. They were financed from Holland, and their arms came from Holland. There was nothing forlorn about their movement, you know. They expected to take over the Government any day, and rule Scotland. All their preaching was pure sedition. The most violent incitement to crime you could imagine. No modern Government could afford to be so patient with such a menace as the Government of the time were. The Covenanters were continually being offered amnesties."

"Well, well. And I thought they were fighting for freedom to worship God their own way."

"No one ever stopped them from worshipping God any way they pleased. What they were out to do was to impose

118

their method of church government not only on Scotland but on England, believe it or not. You should read the Covenant some day. Freedom of worship was not to be allowed to anyone according to the Covenanting creed—except the Covenanters, of course."

"And all those gravestones and monuments that tourists go to see—"

"All Tonypandy. If you ever read on a gravestone that John Whosit 'suffered death for his adherence to the Word of God and Scotland's Covenanted work of Reformation,' with a touching little verse underneath about 'dust sacrificed to tyranny,' you can be sure that the said John Whosit was found guilty before a properly constituted court, of a civil crime punishable by death and that his death had nothing whatever to do with the Word of God." He laughed a little under his breath. "It's the final irony, you know, that a group whose name was anathema to the rest of Scotland in their own time should have been elevated into the position of saints and martyrs."

"I wouldn't wonder if it wasn't onomatopoeic," Carradine said thoughtfully.

"What?"

"Like the Cat and the Rat, you know."

"What are you talking about?"

" 'Member you said, about that Cat and Rat lampoon, that rhyme, that the sound of it made it an offence?"

"Yes; made it venomous."

"Well, the word dragoon does the same thing. I take it that the dragoons were just the policemen of the time."

"Yes. Mounted infantry."

"Well, to me—and I suspect to every other person reading about it—dragoons sound dreadful. They've come to mean something that they never were."

"Yes, I see. Force majeure in being. Actually the Government had only a tiny handful of men to police an enormous area, so the odds were all on the Covenanters' side. In more ways than one. A dragoon (read policeman) couldn't arrest anyone without a warrant (he couldn't stable his horse without the owner's permission, if it comes to that), but there was nothing to hinder a Covenanter lying snug in the heather and picking off dragoons at his leisure. Which they did, of course. And

119

now there's a whole literature about the poor ill-used saint in the heather with his pistol; and the dragoon who died in the course of his duty is a Monster."

"Like Richard."

"Like Richard. How have you been getting on with our own particular Tonypandy?"

"Well, I still haven't managed to find out why Henry was so anxious to hush up that Act was well as repeal it. The thing *was* hushed-up and for years it was forgotten, until the original draft turned up, just by chance, in the Tower records. It was printed in 1611. Speed printed the full text of it in his *History of Great Britain*."

"Oh. So there's no question at all about Titulus Regius. Richard succeeded as the Act says, and the sainted More's account is nonsense. There never was an Elizabeth Lucy in the matter."

"Lucy? Who's Elizabeth Lucy?"

"Oh, I forgot. You weren't on in that act. According to the sainted More, Richard claimed that Edward was married to one of his mistresses, one Elizabeth Lucy."

The disgusted look that the mention of the sainted More always caused on young Carradine's mild face made him look almost nauseated.

"That's nonsense."

"So the sainted More smugly pointed out."

"Why did they want to hide Eleanor Butler?" Carradine said, seeing the point.

"Because she really had married Edward, and the children really were illegitimate. And if the children really were illegitimate, by the way, then no one could rise in their favour and they were no danger to Richard. Have you noticed that the Woodville-Lancastrian invasion was in Henry's favour, and not in the boys'—although Dorset was their half-brother? And that was before any rumours of their non-existence could have reached him. As far as the leaders of the Dorset-Morton rebellion were concerned the boys were of no account. They were backing Henry. That way, Dorset would have a brother-in-law on the throne of England, and the Queen would be his half-sister. Which would be a nice reversal of form for a penniless fugitive."

"Yes. Yes, that's a point, all right; that about Dorset

not fighting to restore his half-brother. If there had been a chance at all that England would have accepted the boy, he surely would have backed the boy. I'll tell you another interesting thing I found. The Queen and her daughters came out of sanctuary quite soon. It's your talking about her son Dorset that reminded me. She not only came out of sanctuary but settled down as if nothing had happened. Her daughters went to festivities at the Palace. And do you know what the pay-off is?"

"No."

"That was *after* the Princes had been 'murdered.' Yes, and I'll tell you something else. With her two boys done to death by their wicked uncle, she writes to her other son, in France—Dorset—and asks him to come home and make his peace with Richard, who will treat him well."

There was silence.

There were no sparrows to talk today. Only the soft sound of the rain against the window.

"No comment," Carradine said at last.

"You know," Grant said, "from the police point of view there is no case against Richard at all. And I mean that literally. It isn't that the case isn't good enough. Good enough to bring into court, I mean. There, quite literally, isn't any case against him at all."

"I'll say there isn't. Especially when I tell you that every single one of those people whose names you sent me were alive and prosperous, and *free,* when Richard was killed at Bosworth. They were not only free, they were very well cared for. Edward's children not only danced at the Palace, they had pensions. He appointed one of the crowd his heir when his own boy died."

"Which one?"

"George's boy."

"So he meant to reverse the attainder on his brother's children."

"Yes. He had protested about his being condemned, if you remember."

"According to even the sainted More, he did. So all the heirs to the throne of England were going about their business, free and unfettered, during the reign of Richard III, the Monster."

"They were more. They were part of the general

scheme of things. I mean, part of the family and the general economy of the realm. I've been reading a collection of York records by a man Davies. Records of the town of York, I mean; not the family. Both young Warwick—George's son—and his cousin, young Lincoln, were members of the Council. The town addressed a letter to them. In 1485, that was. What's more, Richard knighted young Warwick at the same time as he knighted his own son, at a splendid 'do' at York." He paused a long moment, and then blurted out: "Mr. Grant, do you want to write a book about this?"

"A book!" Grant said, astonished. "God forbid. Why?"

"Because I should like to write one. It would make a much better book than the Peasants."

"Write away."

"You see, I'd like to have something to show my father. Pop thinks I'm no good because I can't take an interest in furniture, and marketing, and graphs of sales. If he could actually handle a book that I had written he might believe that I wasn't so hopeless a bet after all. In fact, I wouldn't put it past him to begin to boast about me for a change."

Grant looked at him with benevolence.

"I forgot to ask you what you thought of Crosby Place," he said.

"Oh, fine, fine. If Carradine the Third ever sees it he'll want to take it back with him and rebuild it in the Adirondacks somewhere."

"If you write that book about Richard, he most certainly will. He'll feel like a part-owner. What are you going to call it?"

"The book?"

"Yes."

"I'm going to borrow a phrase from Henry Ford, and call it *History Is the Bunk*."

"Excellent."

"However, I'll have a lot more reading to do and a lot more research, before I can start writing."

"Most assuredly you have. You haven't arrived yet at the real question."

"What is that?"

"Who *did* murder the boys."

"Yes, of course."

"If the boys were alive when Henry took over the Tower what happened to them?"

"Yes. I'll get on to that. I still want to know why it was so important to Henry to hush up the contents of Titulus Regius."

He got up to go, and then noticed the portrait that was lying on its face on the table. He reached over and restored the photograph to its original place, propping it with a concerned care against the pile of books.

"You stay there," he said to the painted Richard. "I'm going to put you back where you belong."

As he went out of the door, Grant said:

"I've just thought of a piece of history which is *not* Tonypandy."

"Yes?" said Carradine, lingering.

"The massacre of Glencoe."

"That really did happen?"

"That really did happen. And—Brent!"

Brent put his head back inside the door.

"Yes?"

"The man who gave the order for it was an ardent Covenanter."

CHAPTER THIRTEEN

Carradine had not been gone more than twenty minutes when Marta appeared, laden with flowers, books, candy, and goodwill. She found Grant deep in the fifteenth century as reported by Sir Cuthbert Oliphant. He greeted her with an absent-mindedness to which she was not accustomed.

"If your two sons had been murdered by your brother-in-law, would you take a handsome pension from him?"

"I take it that the question is rhetorical," Marta said, putting down her sheaf of flowers and looking round to see which of the already occupied vases would best suit their type.

"Honestly, I think historians are all mad. Listen to this:

> The conduct of the Queen-Dowager is hard to explain; whether she feared to be taken from sanctuary by force, or whether she was merely tired of her forlorn existence at Westminster, and had resolved to be reconciled to the murder of her sons out of mere callous apathy, seems uncertain.

"Merciful Heaven!" said Marta, pausing with a delft jar in one hand and a glass cylinder in the other, and looking at him in wild surmise.

"Do you think historians really *listen* to what they are saying?"

"Who was the said Queen-Dowager?"

"Elizabeth Woodville. Edward IV's wife."

"Oh, yes. I played her once. It was a 'bit.' In a play about Warwick the Kingmaker."

124

"Of course I'm only a policeman," Grant said. "Perhaps. I never moved in the right circles. It may be that I've met only nice people. Where would one have to go to meet a woman who became matey with the murderer of her two boys?"

"Greece, I should think," Marta said. *"Ancient* Greece."

"I can't remember a sample even there."

"Or a lunatic asylum, perhaps. Was there any sign of idiocy about Elizabeth Woodville?"

"Not that anyone ever noticed. And she was Queen for twenty years or so."

"Of course the thing is farce, I hope you see," Marta said, going on with her flower arranging. "Not tragedy at all. 'Yes, I know he did kill Edward and little Richard, but he really is a rather charming creature and it is so bad for my rheumatism living in rooms with a north light.' "

Grant laughed, and his good temper came back.

"Yes, of course. It's the height of absurdity. It belongs to Ruthless Rhymes, not to sober history. That is why historians surprise me. They seem to have no talent for the *likeliness* of any situation. They see history like a peepshow; with two-dimensional figures against a distant background."

"Perhaps when you are grubbing about with tattered records you haven't time to learn about people. I don't mean about the people in the records, but just about People. Flesh and blood. And how they react to circumstances."

"How would you play her?" Grant asked, remembering that the understanding of motive was Marta's trade.

"Play who?"

"The woman who came out of sanctuary and made friends with her children's murderer for seven hundred marks per annum and the right to go to parties at the Palace."

"I couldn't. There is no such woman outside Euripides or a delinquent's home. One could only play her as a rag. She'd make a very good burlesque, now I think of it. A take-off of poetic tragedy. The blank verse kind. I must try it sometime. For a charity matinée, or something. I hope you don't hate mimosa. It's odd, considering how

125

long I've known you, how little I know your likes and dislikes. Who invented the woman who became buddies with her sons' murderer?"

"No one invented her. Elizabeth Woodville did come out of sanctuary, and did accept a pension from Richard. The pension was not only granted, it was paid. Her daughters went to parties at the Palace and she wrote to her other son—her first-marriage son—to come home from France and make his peace with Richard. Oliphant's only suggestion as to the reason for this is that she was either frightened of being dragged out of sanctuary (did you ever know of anyone who was dragged out of sanctuary? The man who did that would be excommunicated—and Richard was a very good son of Holy Church) or that she was bored with sanctuary life."

"And what is your theory about so odd a proceeding?"

"The obvious explanation is that the boys were alive and well. No one at that time ever suggested otherwise."

Marta considered the sprays of mimosa. "Yes, of course. You said that there was no accusation in that Bill of Attainder. After Richard's death, I mean." Her eyes went from the mimosa to the portrait on the table and then to Grant. "You think, then, you really soberly think, as a policeman, that Richard didn't have anything to do with the boys' deaths."

"I'm quite sure that they were alive and well when Henry took over the Tower on his arrival in London. There is *nothing* that would explain his omission to make a scandal of it if the boys were missing. Can you think of anything?"

"No. No, of course not. It is quite inexplicable. I have always taken it for granted that there was a terrific scandal about it. That it would be one of the main accusations against Richard. You and my woolly lamb seem to be having a lovely time with history. When I suggested a little investigation to pass the time and stop the prickles I had no idea that I was contributing to the rewriting of history. Which reminds me, Atlanta Shergold is gunning for you."

"For me? I've never even met her."

"Nevertheless she is looking for you with a gun. She says that Brent's attitude to the B.M. has become the attitude of an addict to his drug. She can't drag him away

126

from it. If she takes him away from it physically, he spends the time harking back to it in his mind; so that she mightn't exist as far as he is concerned. He has even stopped sitting through *To Sea in a Bowl*. Do you see much of him?"

"He was here a few minutes before you came. But I don't expect to hear from him again for some days to come."

But in that he was wrong.

Just before supper-time the porter appeared with a telegram.

Grant put his thumb under the dainty Post Office lick on the flap and extracted two sheets of telegram. The telegram was from Brent.

Hell and damnation an awful thing has happened (stop) you know that chronicle in Latin I talked about (stop) the chronicle written by the monk at Croyland Abbey (stop) well I've just seen it and the rumour is there the rumour about the boys being dead (stop) the thing is written before Richard's death so we are sunk aren't we and I specially am sunk and that fine book of mine will never be written (stop) is anyone allowed to commit suicide in your river or is it reserved for the British

Brent

Into the silence the voice of the porter said: "It's reply-paid, sir. Do you want to send an answer?"

"What? Oh. No. Not right away. I'll send it down presently."

"Very good, sir," said the porter looking respectfully at the two sheets of telegram—in the porter's family a telegram was confined to one sheet only—and went away, not humming this time.

Grant considered the news conveyed with such trans-atlantic extravagance in the matter of telegraphic communication. He read the thing again.

"Croyland," he said, considering. Why did that ring a bell? No one had mentioned Croyland so far in this case. Carradine had talked merely of a monkish chronicle somewhere.

He had been too often, in his professional life, faced with a fact that apparently destroyed his whole case to be dismayed now. He reacted as he would have reacted in a professional investigation. He took out the upsetting small fact and looked at it. Calmly. Dispassionately. With none of poor Carradine's wild dismay.

"Croyland," he said again. Croyland was somewhere in Cambridgeshire. Or was it Norfolk? Somewhere on the borders there, in the flat country.

The Midget came in with his supper, and propped the flat bowl-like plate where he could eat from it with a modicum of comfort, but he was not aware of her.

"Can you reach your pudding easily from there?" she asked. And as he did not answer: "Mr. Grant, can you reach your pudding if I leave it on the edge there?"

"*Ely!*" he shouted at her.

"What?"

"Ely," he said; softly, to the ceiling.

"Mr. Grant, aren't you feeling well?"

He became conscious of The Midget's well-powdered and concerned little face as it intruded between him and the familiar cracks.

"I'm fine, fine. Better than I've ever been in my life. Wait just a moment, there's a good girl, and send a telegram down for me. Give me my writing-pad. I can't reach it with that mess of rice pudding in the way."

She gave him the pad and pencil, and on the reply-paid form he wrote:

Can you find me a similar rumour in France at about the same date?

Grant

After that he ate his supper with a good appetite, and settled down to a good night's sleep. He was floating in that delicious half-way stage on the way to unconsciousness when he became aware that someone was leaning over to inspect him. He opened his eyes to see who it might be, and looked straight into the anxious yearning brown irises of The Amazon, looking larger and more cowlike than ever in the soft lamplight. She was holding in her hand a yellow envelope.

"I didn't quite know what to do," she said. "I didn't want to disturb you and yet I didn't know whether it mightn't be important. A telegram, you know. You never can tell. And if you didn't have it tonight it would mean a whole twelve hours' delay. Nurse Ingham has gone off duty, so there was no one to ask till Nurse Briggs comes on at ten. I hope I haven't wakened you up. But you weren't really asleep, were you?"

Grant assured her that she had done the right thing and she let out a sigh that nearly blew the portrait of Richard over. She stood by while he read the telegram, with an air of being ready to support him in any evil news that it might contain. To The Amazon all telegrams conveyed evil tidings.

The telegram was from Carradine.

It said: "You mean you want repeat want that there should be another repeat another accusation question-mark—Brent."

Grant took the reply-paid form and wrote: "Yes. Preferably in France."

Then he said to The Amazon: "You can turn out the light, I think. I'm going to sleep until seven tomorrow morning."

He fell asleep wondering how long it would be before he saw Carradine again, and what the odds were against that much desired instance of a second rumour.

But it was not so long after all until Carradine turned up again, and he turned up looking anything but suicidal. Indeed he seemed in some queer way to have broadened out. His coat seemed less of an appendage and more of a garment. He beamed at Grant.

"Mr. Grant, you're a wonder. Do they have more like you at Scotland Yard? Or do you rate special?"

Grant looked at him almost unbelieving. "Don't tell me you've turned up a French instance!"

"Didn't you want me to?"

"Yes. But I hardly dared hope for it. The odds against seemed tremendous. What form did the rumour take in France? A chronicle? A letter?"

"No. Something much more surprising. Something much more dismaying, actually. It seems that the Chancellor of France, in a speech to the States-General at
129

Tours, spoke of the rumour. Indeed he was quite eloquent about it. In a way, his eloquence was the one scrap of comfort I could find in the situation."

"Why?"

"Well, it sounded more to my mind like a Senator being hasty about someone who had brought in a measure his own people back home wouldn't like. More like politics than State, if you know what I mean."

"You should be at the Yard, Brent. What did the Chancellor say?"

"Well, it's in French and my French isn't very good so perhaps you'd better read it for yourself."

He handed over a sheet of his childish writing and Grant read:

Regardez, je vous prie, les événements qui après la mort du roi Edouard sont arrivés dans ce pays. Contemplez ses enfants, déjà grands et braves, massacrés impunément, et la couronne transportée à l'assassin par la faveur des peuples.

" 'Ce pays,' " said Grant. "Then he was in full flood against England. He even suggests that it was with the will of the English people that the boys were 'massacred.' We are being held up as a barbarous race."

"Yes. That's what I meant. It's a Congressman scoring a point. Actually, the French Regency sent an embassy to Richard that same year—about six months later—so they had probably found that the rumour wasn't true. Richard signed a safe-conduct for their visit. He wouldn't have done that if they had been still slanging him as a murdering untouchable."

"No. Can you give me the dates of the two libels?"

"Sure. I have them here. The monk at Croyland wrote about events in the late summer of 1483. He says that there was a rumour that the boys had been put to death but no one knew how. The nasty slap in the meeting of the States-General was in January 1484."

"Perfect," said Grant.

"*Why* did you want there to have been another instance of rumour?"

"As a cross-check. Do you know where Croyland is?"

"Yes. In the Fen country."

"In the Fen country. Near Ely. And it was in the Fen country that Morton was hiding out after his escape from Buckingham's charge."

"Morton! Yes, of course."

"If Morton was the carrier, then there had to be another outbreak on the Continent, when he moved on there. Morton escaped from England in the autumn of 1483, and the rumour appears promptly in January 1484. Croyland is a very isolated place, incidentally; it would be an ideal place for a fugitive bishop to hide out till he could arrange transport abroad."

"Morton!" said Carradine again, rolling the name over on his tongue. "Wherever there's hanky-panky in this business you stub your toe against Morton."

"So you've noticed that too."

"He was the heart of that conspiracy to murder Richard before he could be crowned, he was in the back of the rebellion against Richard once he *was* crowned, and his trail to the Continent is sticky as a snail's with—with subversion."

"We-ll, the snail part is mere deduction. It wouldn't stand up in court. But there's no peradventure about his activities once he was across the channel. He settled down to a whole-time job of subversion. He and a buddy of his called Christopher Urswick worked like beavers in Henry's interest; 'sending preuie letters and cloked messengers' to England to stir up hostility to Richard."

"Yes? I don't know as much as you about what stands up in court and what won't but it seems to me that that snail's trail is a very allowable deduction—if you'll allow me. I don't suppose Morton waited till he was overseas before beginning his undermining."

"No. No, of course he didn't. It was life and death to Morton that Richard should go. Unless Richard went, John Morton's career was over. He was finished. It wasn't even that there would be no preferment for him now. There would be nothing. He would be stripped of his numerous livings and be reduced to his plain priest's frock. He, John Morton. Who had been within touching distance of an archbishopric. But if he could help Henry Tudor to a throne then he might still become not only Archbishop of Canterbury but a Cardinal besides. Oh, yes; it was desperately, overwhelmingly important to Morton that Richard should not have the governing of England."

"Well," said Brent, "he was the right man for a job of subversion. I don't suppose he knew what a scruple was. A little rumour like infanticide must have been child's play to him."

"There's always the odd chance that he believed it, of course," Grant said, his habit of weighing evidence overcoming even his dislike of Morton.

"Believed that the boys were murdered?"

"Yes. It may have been someone else's invention. After all, the country must have been swarming with Lancastrian tales, part mere ill-will, part propaganda. He may have been merely passing on the latest sample."

"Huh! I wouldn't put it past him to be paving the way for their future murder," Brent said tartly.

Grant laughed. "I wouldn't, at that," he said. "What else did you get from your monk at Croyland?"

"A little comfort, too. I found after I had written that panic wire to you that he wasn't at all to be taken as gospel. He just put down what gossip came his way from the outer world. He says, for instance, that Richard had a second coronation, at York; and that of course just isn't true. If he can be wrong about a big, known, fact like a coronation, then he's not to be trusted as a reporter. But he *did* know about Titulus Regius, by the way. He recorded the whole tenor of it, including Lady Eleanor."

"That's interesting. Even a monk at Croyland had heard who Edward was supposed to have been married to."

"Yes. The sainted More must have dreamed up Elizabeth Lucy a good deal later."

"To say nothing of the unspeakable story that Richard based his claim on his mother's shame."

"What?"

"He says that Richard caused a sermon to be preached claiming that Edward and George were his mother's sons by some other father, and that he, Richard, was the only

132

legitimate son and therefore the only true heir."

"The sainted More might have thought up a more convincing one," young Carradine said dryly.

"Yes. Especially when Richard was living in his mother's house at the time of the libel!"

"So he was. I'd forgotten that. I don't have a proper police brain. That's very neat, what you say about Morton being the carrier of the rumour. But suppose the rumour turns up somewhere else, even yet."

"It's possible, of course. But I'm willing to lay you fifties to any amount that it won't. I don't for one moment believe that there was any general rumour that the boys were missing."

"Why not?"

"For a reason that I hold to be unanswerable. If there had been any general uneasiness, any obviously subversive rumours or action, Richard would have taken immediate steps to checkmate them. When the rumour went round, later, that he was proposing to marry his niece Elizabeth—the boys' eldest sister—he was on to it like a hawk. He not only sent letters to the various towns denying the rumour in no uncertain terms, he was so furious (and evidently thought it of such importance that he should not be traduced) that he summoned the 'heid yins' of London to the biggest hall he could find (so that he could get them all in at one time) and told them face to face what he thought about the affair."

"Yes. Of course you're right. Richard would have made a public denial of the rumour if the rumour was general. After all, it was a much more horrifying one than the one that he was going to marry his niece."

"Yes; actually you could get a dispensation to marry your niece in those days. Perhaps you still can, for all I know. That's not my department at the Yard. What is certain is that if Richard went to such length to contradict the marriage rumour then he most certainly would have gone to much greater lengths to put a stop to the murder one, if it had existed. The conclusion is inevitable: there *was* no general rumour of disappearance or foul play where the boys were concerned."

"Just a thin little trickle between the Fens and France."

"Just a thin little trickle between the Fens and France. Nothing in the picture suggests any worry about the boys. I mean: in a police investigation you look for any abnormalities in behaviour among the suspects in a crime. Why did X, who always goes to the movies on a Thursday night, decide on that night of all nights not to go? Why did Y take a return half as usual and very unusually not use it? That sort of thing. But in the short time between Richard's succession and his death everyone behaves quite normally. The boys' mother comes out of sanctuary and makes her peace with Richard. The girls resume their court life. The boys are presumably still doing the lessons that their father's death had interrupted. Their young cousins have a place on the Council and are of sufficient importance for the town of York to be addressing letters to them. It's all quite a normal, peaceful scene, with everyone going about their ordinary business, and no suggestion anywhere that a spectacular and unnecessary murder has just taken place in the family."

"It looks as if I might write that book after all, Mr. Grant."

"Most certainly you will write it. You have not only Richard to rescue from calumny; you have to clear Elizabeth Woodville of the imputation of condoning her sons' murder for seven hundred marks a year and perks."

"I can't write the book and leave it in the air like that, of course. I'll *have* to have at least a theory as to what became of the boys."

"You will."

Carradine's mild gaze came away from the small woolly clouds over the Thames and considered Grant with a question in it.

"Why that tone?" he asked. "Why are you looking like a cat with cream?"

"Well, I've been proceeding along police lines. During those empty days while I was waiting for you to turn up again."

"Police lines?"

"Yes. Who benefits, and all that. We've discovered that it wouldn't be a pin's-worth of advantage to Richard that the boys should die. So we go on looking round to see whom, in that case, it *would* benefit. And this is where Titulus Regius comes in."

"What has Titulus Regius got to do with the murder?"

"Henry VII married the boys' eldest sister. Elizabeth."

"Yes."

"By way of reconciling the Yorkists to his occupation of the throne."

"Yes."

"By repealing Titulus Regius, he made her legitimate."

"Sure."

"But by making the children legitimate he automatically made the two boys heir to the throne before her. In fact, by repealing Titulus Regius he made the elder of the two King of England."

Carradine made a little clicking sound with his tongue. His eyes behind their horn-rims were glowing with pleasure.

"So," said Grant, "I propose that we proceed with investigation along those lines."

"Sure. What do you want?"

"I want to know a lot more about that confession of Tyrrel's. But first, and most of all, I'd like to know how the people concerned acted. What happened to them; not what anyone reported of anyone. Just as we did in the case of Richard's succession after Edward's unexpected death."

"Fine. What do you want to know?"

"I want to know what became of all the York heirs that Richard left so alive and well and prosperous. Every single one of them. Can you do that for me?"

"Sure. That's elementary."

"And I could bear to know more about Tyrrel. About the man himself, I mean. Who he was, and what he had done."

"I'll do that." Carradine got up with such an on-with-the-charge air that for one moment Grant thought that he was actually going to button his coat. "Mr. Grant, I'm so grateful to you for all this—this—"

"This fun and games?"

"When you're on your feet again, I'll—I'll—I'll take you round the Tower of London."

"Make it Greenwich-and-back by boat. Our island Race have a passion for the nautical."

"How long do they reckon it will be before you're out of bed, do you know?"

"I'll probably be up before you come back with the news about the heirs and Tyrrel."

CHAPTER FOURTEEN

Grant was not, as it happened, out of bed when Carradine came again, but he was sitting up.

"You can't imagine," he said to Brent, "how fascinating the opposite wall looks, after the ceiling. And how small and queer the world looks right way up."

He was touched by Carradine's obvious pleasure in this progress and it was some time before they got down to business. It was Grant who had to say: "Well, how did the York heirs make out under Henry VII?"

"Oh, yes," said the boy, pulling out his usual wad of notes and drawing up a chair by hooking his right toe in the crossbar. He sat down on the chair. "Where shall I begin?"

"Well, about Elizabeth we know. He married her, and she was Queen of England until she died and he made a bid for the mad Juana of Spain."

"Yes. She was married to Henry in the spring of 1486—in January, rather; five months after Bosworth —and she died in the spring of 1503."

"Seventeen years. Poor Elizabeth. With Henry it must have seemed like seventy. He was what is euphemistically referred to as 'unuxorious.' Let us go on down the family. Edward's children, I mean. Fate of the two boys unknown. What happened to Cicely?"

"She was married to his old uncle Lord Welles, and sent away to live in Lincolnshire. Anne and Katherine, who were children, were married when they were old enough to good Lancastrians. Bridget, the youngest, became a nun at Dartford."

"Orthodox enough, so far. Who comes next? George's boy."

"Yes. Young Warwick. Shut up for life in the Tower, and executed for allegedly planning to escape."

"So. And George's daughter? Margaret."

"She became the Countess of Salisbury. Her execution by Henry VIII on a trumped-up charge is apparently the classic sample of judicial murder."

"Elizabeth's son? The alternative heir?"

"John de la Pole. He went to live with his aunt in Burgundy until—"

"To live with Margaret, Richard's sister."

"Yes. He died in the Simnel rising. But he had a younger brother that you didn't put in that list. He was executed by Henry VIII. He had surrendered to Henry VII under a safe-conduct, so Henry, I suppose, thought that it might break his luck to ignore that. In any case he had about used up his quota. Henry VIII took no chances. He didn't stop at De la Pole. There were four more that you missed out of that list. Exeter, Surrey, Buckingham, and Montague. He got rid of the lot."

"And Richard's son? John? The bastard one."

"Henry VII granted him a pension of £20 a year, but he was the first of the lot to go."

"On what charge?"

"On having been suspected of receiving an invitation to go to Ireland."

"You're joking."

"I'm not. Ireland was the focus of loyalist rebellion. The York family were very popular in Ireland, and to get an invitation from that direction was as good as a death warrant in Henry's eyes. Though I can't think why even Henry would have bothered about young John. 'An active, well-disposed boy,' he was, by the way, according to the 'Foedera.' "

"His claim was better than Henry's," Grant said, very tart. "He was the illegitimate only son of a King. Henry was the great-grandson of an illegitimate son of a younger son of a King."

There was silence for some time.

Then Carradine, out of the silence, said: "Yes."

"Yes to what?"

"To what you are thinking."

"It does look like it, doesn't it? They're the only two who are missing from the list."

There was another silence.

"They were all judicial murders," Grant said presently. "Murders under the form of law. But you can't bring a capital charge against a pair of children."

"No," agreed Carradine, and went on watching the sparrows. "No, it would have to be done some other way. After all, they were the important ones."

"The vital ones."

"How do we start?"

"As we did with Richard's succession. Find out where everyone was in the first months of Henry's reign and what they were doing. Say the first year of his reign. There will be a break in the pattern somewhere, just as there was a break in the preparations for the boy's coronation."

"Right."

"Did you find out anything about Tyrrel? Who he was?"

"Yes. He wasn't at all what I had imagined. I'd imagined him as a sort of hanger-on; hadn't you?"

"Yes, I think I did. Wasn't he?"

"No. He was a person of importance. He was Sir James Tyrrel of Gipping. He had been on various—committees, I suppose you'd call them, for Edward IV. And he was created a Knight Banneret, whatever that is, at the siege of Berwick. And he did well for himself under Richard, though I can't find that he was at the battle of Bosworth. A lot of people came too late for the battle—did you know?—so I don't suppose that means anything particular. Anyhow, he wasn't that lackey-on-the-make person that I'd always pictured."

"That's interesting. How did he make out under Henry VII?"

"Well, that's the *really* interesting thing. For such a very good and successful servant of the York family, he seems to have fairly blossomed under Henry. Henry appointed him Constable of Guisnes. Then he was sent as ambassador to Rome. He was one of the Commissioners for negotiating the Treaty of Etaples. And Henry gave him a grant for life of the revenues of some lands in Wales, but made him exchange them for revenues of the county of Guisnes of equal value—I can't think why."

"I can," said Grant.

"You can?"

"Has it struck you that all his honours and his commissions are outside England? Even the reward of land revenues."

"Yes, so they are. What does that convey to you?"

"Nothing at the moment. Perhaps he just found Guisnes better for his bronchial catarrh. It is possible to read too much into historical transactions. Like Shakespeare's plays, they are capable of almost endless interpretations. How long did this honeymoon with Henry VII last?"

"Oh, quite a long time. Everything was just grand until 1502."

"What happened in 1502?"

"Henry heard that he had been ready to help one of the York crowd in the Tower to escape to Germany. He sent the whole garrison of Calais to besiege the castle at Guisnes. That wasn't quick enough for him, so he sent his Lord Privy Seal—know what that is?"

Grant nodded.

"Sent his Lord Privy Seal—what names you English have dreamed up for your Elks officials—to offer him safe conduct if he would come aboard a ship at Calais and confer with the Chancellor of the Exchequer."

"Don't tell me."

"I don't need to, do I? He finished up in a dungeon in the Tower. And was beheaded 'in great haste and without trial' on May 6, 1502."

"And what about his confession?"

"There wasn't one."

"What!"

"Don't look at me like that. I'm not responsible."

"But I thought he confessed to the murder of the boys."

"Yes, according to various accounts. But they are accounts of a confession, not—not a transcript, if you see what I mean."

"You mean, Henry didn't publish a confession?"

"No. His paid historian, Polydore Virgil, gave an account of how the murder was done. After Tyrrel was dead."

"But if Tyrrel confessed that he murdered the boys at Richard's instigation, why wasn't he charged with the crime and publicly tried for it?"

"I can't imagine."

"Let me get this straight. Nothing was heard of Tyrrel's confession until Tyrrel was dead."

"No."

"Tyrrel confesses that way back in 1483, nearly twenty years ago, he pelted up to London from Warwick, got the keys of the Tower from the Constable—I forget his name—"

"Brackenbury. Sir Robert Brackenbury."

"Yes. Got the keys of the Tower from Sir Robert Brackenbury for one night, murdered the boys, handed back the keys, and reported back to Richard. He confesses this, and so puts an end to what must have been a much canvassed mystery, and yet nothing public is done with him."

"Not a thing."

"I'd hate to go into court with a story like that."

"I wouldn't even consider it, myself. It's as phoney a tale as ever I heard."

"Didn't they even bring Brackenbury in to affirm or deny the story of the keys being handed over?"

"Brackenbury was killed at Bosworth."

"So he was conveniently dead too, was he?" He lay and thought about it. "You know, if Brackenbury died at Bosworth, then we have one more small piece of evidence on our side."

"How? What?"

"If that had really happened; I mean: if the keys were handed over for a night on Richard's order, then a lot of junior officials at the Tower must have been aware of it. It is quite inconceivable that one or other of them wouldn't be ready to tell the tale to Henry when he took over the Tower. Especially if the boys were missing. Brackenbury was dead. Richard was dead. The next in command at the Tower would be expected to produce the boys. When they weren't producible, he *must* have said: 'The Constable handed over the keys, one night, and since then the boys have not been seen.' There would have been the most ruthless hue and cry after the man who had been given the

141

keys. He would have been Exhibit A in the case against Richard, and to produce him would have been a feather in Henry's cap."

"Not only that, but Tyrrel was too well known to the people at the Tower to have passed unrecognised. In the small London of that day he must have been quite a well-known figure."

"Yes. If that story were true Tyrrel would have been tried and executed for the boys' murder, openly, in 1485. He had no one to protect him." He reached for his cigarettes. "So what we're left with is that Henry executed Tyrrel in 1502, and then announced by way of his tame historians that Tyrrel had confessed that twenty years before he had murdered the Princes."

"Yes."

"And he didn't offer, anywhere, at any time, any reason for trying Tyrrel for this atrocious thing he had confessed."

"No. Not as far as I can make out. He was sideways as a crab, you know. He never went straight at anything, even murder. It had to be covered up to look like something else. He waited years to find some sort of legal excuse that would camouflage a murder. He had a mind like a cork-screw. Do you know what his first official action as Henry VII was?"

"No."

"To execute some of the men fighting for Richard at Bosworth *on a charge of treason*. And do you know how he managed to make it legally treason? By dating his reign from the day before Bosworth. A mind that was capable of a piece of sharp practice of that calibre was capable of anything." He took the cigarette that Grant was offering him. "But he didn't get away with it," he added, with sober joy. "Oh, no, he didn't get away with it. The English, bless them, drew the line at that. They told him where he got off."

"How?"

"They presented him, in that nice polite English way, with an Act of Parliament that said that no one serving the Sovereign Lord of the land for the time being should be convicted of treason or suffer either forfeiture or imprisonment, and they made him consent to it. That's terribly English, that ruthless politeness. No yelling in the street or throwing stones because they didn't like his little bit of cheating. Just a nice polite reasonable Act for him to swallow and like it. I bet he did a slow burn about that one. Well, I must be on my way. It's sure nice to see you sitting up and taking notice. We'll be having that trip to Greenwich in no time at all, I see. What's at Greenwich?"

"Some very fine architecture and a fine stretch of muddy river."

"That all?"

"And some good pubs."

"We're going to Greenwich."

When he had gone Grant slid down in bed and smoked one cigarette after another while he considered the tale of those heirs of York who had prospered under Richard III, and gone to their graves under Henry VII.

Some of them may have "asked for it." Carradine's report had, after all, been a précis; innocent of qualification, insusceptible to half-tones. But it was surely a thundering great coincidence that *all* the lives who stood between the Tudors and the throne had been cut short so conveniently.

He looked, with no great enthusiasm, at the book that young Carradine had brought him. It was called *The Life and Reign of Richard III*, by someone James Gairdner. Carradine had assured him that he would find Dr. Gairdner well worth his while. Dr. Gairdner was, according to Brent, "a scream."

The book did not appear to Grant to be markedly hilarious, but anything about Richard was better than something about anyone else, so he began to glance through it, and presently he became aware just what Brent had meant by saying that the good Doctor was a "scream." Dr. Gairdner obstinately believed Richard to be a murderer, but since he was a writer honest, learned, and according to his lights impartial, it was not in him to suppress facts. The spectacle of Dr. Gairdner trying to make his facts fit his theory was the most entertaining thing in gymnastics that Grant had witnessed for some time.

Dr. Gairdner acknowledged with no apparent sense of incongruity Richard's great wisdom, his generosity, and his courage, his ability, his charm, his popularity, and the

143

trust that he inspired even in his beaten enemies; and in the same breath reported his vile slander of his mother and his slaughter of two helpless children. Tradition says, said the worthy Doctor; and solemnly reported the horrible tradition and subscribed to it. There was nothing mean or paltry in his character, according to the Doctor—but he was a murderer of innocent children. Even his enemies had confidence in his justice—but he murdered his own nephews. His integrity was remarkable—but he killed for gain.

As a contortionist Dr. Gairdner was the original boneless wonder. More than ever Grant wondered with what part of their brains historians reasoned. It was certainly by no process of reasoning known to ordinary mortals that they arrived at their conclusions. Nowhere in life had he met any human being remotely resembling either Dr. Gairdner's Richard or Oliphant's Elizabeth Woodville.

Perhaps there was something in Laura's theory that human nature found it difficult to give up preconceived beliefs. That there was some vague inward opposition to, and resentment of, a reversal of accepted fact. Certainly Dr. Gairdner dragged like a frightened child on the hand that was pulling him towards the inevitable.

That charming men of great integrity had committed murder in their day Grant knew only too well. But not that kind of murder and not for that kind of reason. The kind of man whom Dr. Gairdner had drawn in his *Life and History of Richard III* would commit murder only when his own personal life had been *bouleversé* by some earthquake. He would murder his wife for unfaithfulness suddenly discovered, perhaps. Or kill the partner whose secret speculation had ruined their firm and the future of his children. Whatever murder he committed would be the result of acute emotion, it would never be planned; and it would never be a base murder.

One could not say: Because Richard possessed this quality and that, therefore he was incapable of murder. But one could say: Because Richard possessed these qualities, therefore he is incapable of this murder.

It would have been a silly murder, that murder of the boy Princes; and Richard was a remarkably able man. It was base beyond description; and he was a man of great

144

integrity. It was callous; and he was noted for his warm-heartedness.

One could go through the catalogue of his acknowledged virtues, and find that each of them, individually, made his part in the murder unlikely in the extreme. Taken together they amounted to a wall of impossibility that towered into fantasy.

CHAPTER FIFTEEN

"There was one person you forgot to ask for," Carradine said, breezing in, very gay, some days later. "In your list of kind inquiries."

"Hullo. Who was that?"

"Stillington."

"Of course! The worthy Bishop of Bath. If Henry hated Titulus Regius, as a witness of Richard's integrity and his own wife's illegitimacy, he must still more have disliked the presence of its instigator. What happened to old Stillington? Judicial murder?"

"Apparently the old boy wouldn't play."

"Wouldn't play what?"

"Henry's pet game. Out goes he. Either he was a wily old bird, or he was too innocent to see the snare at all. It's my belief—if a mere Research Worker is entitled to a belief—that he was so innocent that no agent provocateur could provoke him to anything. Not anything that could be made a capital charge, anyhow."

"Are you telling me that he defeated Henry?"

"No. Oh, no. No one ever defeated Henry. Henry put him on a charge and conveniently forgot to release him. And never home came he. Who was that? Mary on the sands of Dee?"

"You're very bright this morning, not to say exhilarated."

"Don't say it in that suspicious tone. They're not open yet. This effervescence that you observe in me is intellectual carbonisation. Spiritual rejoicing. An entirely cerebral scintillation."

"Well? Sit down and cough up. What is so good? I take it that something is?"

"Good is hardly the proper word. It's beautiful, perfectly-holy beautiful."

"I think you *have* been drinking."

"I couldn't drink this morning if I tried. I'm bung full, full up to the gullet's edge, with satisfaction."

"I take it you found that break in the pattern we were looking for."

"Yes, I found it, but it was later than we had thought. Later in time, I mean. Further on. In the first months everyone did what you would expect them to do. Henry took over—not a word about the boys—and cleaned up, got married to the boys' sister. Got his own attainder reversed by a Parliament of his own attainted followers—no mention of the boys—and got an act of attainder through against Richard and his loyal subjects whose service was so neatly made treason by that one day's ante-dating. That brought a fine heap of forfeited estates into the kitty in one go. The Croyland monk was terribly scandalised, by the way, at Henry's sharp practice in the matter of treason. 'O God,' he says, 'what security are our kings to have henceforth in the day of battle if their loyal followers may in defeat be deprived of life, fortune, and inheritance?' "

"He reckoned without his countrymen."

"Yes. He might have known that the English would get round to that matter sooner or later. Perhaps he was an alien. Anyhow, everything went on just as you would expect things to go with Henry in charge. He succeeded in August of 1485, and married Elizabeth in the following January. Elizabeth had her first child at Winchester, and her mother was there with her and was present at the baptism. That was in September 1486. Then she came back to London—the Queen Dowager, I mean—in the autumn. And in February—hold on to everything—in February she was shut up in a convent for the rest of her life."

"*Elizabeth Woodville?*" Grant said, in the greatest astonishment. This was the very last thing he had expected.

"Yes. Elizabeth Woodville. The boys' mother."

"How do you know that she didn't go voluntarily?" Grant asked, when he had thought of it for a little. "It was not an uncommon thing for great ladies who were tired of court life to retire into an Order. It was not a severe existence, you know. Indeed, I have an idea it was fairly comfortable for rich women."

"Henry stripped her of everything she owned, and ordered her into the nunnery at Bermondsey. And that, by the way, *did* create a sensation. There was 'much wondering,' it appears."

"I'm not surprised. What an extraordinary thing. Did he give a reason?"

"Yes."

"What did he say he was ruining her for?"

"For being nice to Richard."

"Are you serious?"

"Sure."

"Is that the official wording?"

"No. That's the version of Henry's pet historian."

"Virgil?"

"Yes. The actual order of council that shut her up, said it was 'for various considerations.' "

"Are you quoting?" asked Grant, incredulous.

"I'm quoting. That's what it said: 'For various considerations.' "

After a moment Grant said: "He had no talent for excuses, had he? In his place I would have thought up six better ones."

"Either he couldn't be bothered or he thought other people very credulous. Mark you, her niceness to Richard didn't worry him until eighteen months after he succeeded Richard. Up till then everything had apparently been smooth as milk. He had even given her presents, manors and what not, when he succeeded Richard."

"What was his real reason? Have you any suggestion?"

"Well, I've another little item that may give you ideas. It certainly gave me one hell of a big idea."

"Go on."

"In June of that year—"

"Which year?"

"The first year of Elizabeth's marriage. 1486. The year when she was married in January and had Prince Arthur at Winchester in September, with her mother dancing attendance."

"All right. Yes."

"In June of that year, Sir James Tyrrel received a general pardon. On the 16th June."

"But that means very little, you know. It was quite a usual thing. At the end of a period of service. Or on setting out on a new one. It merely meant that you were quit of anything that anyone might think of raking up against you afterwards."

"Yes, I know. I know that. The first pardon isn't the surprising one."

"The *first* pardon? Was there a second one?"

"Yes. That's the pay-off. There was a second general pardon to Sir James exactly a month later. To be exact on the 16th July, 1486."

"Yes," Grant said, thinking it over. "That really is extraordinary."

"It's highly unusual, anyway. I asked an old boy who works next to me at the B.M.—he does historical research and he's been a wonderful help to me I don't mind telling you—and he said he had never come across another instance. I showed him the two entries—in the *Memorials of Henry VII*—and he mooned over them like a lover."

Grant said, considering: "On the 16th June, Tyrrel is given a general pardon. On the 16th July he is given a second general pardon. In November or thereabouts the boys' mother comes back to town. And in February she is immured for life."

"Suggestive?"

"Very."

"You think he did it? Tyrrel."

"It could be. It's very suggestive, isn't it, that when we find the break in the normal pattern that we've been looking for, Tyrrel is there, on the spot, with a most unconscionable break in his own pattern. When did the rumour that the boys were missing first become general? I mean, something to be talked openly about."

"Quite early in Henry's reign, it would seem."

"Yes; it fits. It would certainly explain the thing that has puzzled us from the beginning in this affair."

"What do you mean?"

"It would explain why there was no fuss when the boys disappeared. It's always been a puzzling thing, even to people who thought that Richard did it. Indeed, when you

149

come to think of it it would be impossible for Richard to get away with it. There was a large, and very active, and very powerful opposition party in Richard's day, and he left them all free and scattered up and down the country to carry on as they liked. He had all the Woodville-Lancaster crowd to deal with if the boys had gone missing. But where interference or undue curiosity was concerned Henry was sitting pretty. Henry had got *his* opposition party safely in jail. The only possible danger was his mother-in-law, and at the very moment when she becomes capable of being a prying nuisance she too is put under hatches and battened down."

"Yes. Wouldn't you think that there was *something* she could have done? When she found that she was being prevented from getting news of the boys."

"She may never have known that they were missing. He may just have said: 'It is my wish that you should not see them. I think you are a bad influence on them: you who came out of sanctuary and let your daughters go to that man's parties!"

"Yes, that's so, of course. He didn't have to wait until she actually became suspicious. The whole thing might have been one move. 'You're a bad woman, and a bad mother; I am sending you into a convent to save your soul and your children from the contamination of your presence.' "

"Yes. And where the rest of England were concerned, he was as safe as any murderer ever could be. After his happy thought about the 'treason' accusation, no one was going to stick his neck out by inquiring particularly about the boys' health. Everyone must have been walking on eggs as it was. No one knowing what Henry might think of next to make into a restrospective offence that would send their lives into limbo and their estates into Henry's kitty. No, it was no time to be overcurious about anything that didn't directly concern oneself. Not that it would be easy, in any case, to satisfy one's curiosity."

"With the boys living at the Tower, you mean."

"With the boys living in a Tower officialled by Henry's men. There was none of Richard's get-together live-and-let-live attitude about Henry. No York-Lancaster alliance

150

for Henry. The people at the Tower would be Henry's men."

"Yes. Of course they would. Did you know that Henry was the first English King to have a bodyguard? I wonder what he told his wife about her brothers."

"Yes. That would be interesting to know. He may even have told her the truth."

"*Henry!* Never! It would cost Henry a spiritual struggle, Mr. Grant, to acknowledge that two and two were four. I tell you, he was a crab; he never went straight at anything."

"If he were sadist he could tell her with impunity, you know. There was practically nothing she could do about it. Even if she wanted to. She mightn't have wanted to all that much. She had just produced an heir to the throne of England and was getting ready to produce another. She might not have the spare interest for a crusade; especially a crusade that would knock the ground from under her own feet."

"He wasn't a sadist, Henry," young Carradine said sadly. Sad at having to grant Henry even a negative virtue. "In a way he was just the opposite. He didn't enjoy murder at all. He had to pretty it up before he could bear the thought of it. Dress it up in legal ribbons. If you think that Henry got a kick out of boasting to Elizabeth in bed about what he had done with her brothers, I think you're wrong."

"Yes, probably," Grant said. And lay thinking about Henry. "I've just thought of the right adjective for Henry," he said presently. "Shabby. He was a shabby creature."

"Yes. Even his hair was thin and scanty."

"I didn't mean it physically."

"I know you didn't."

"Everything that he did was shabby. Come to think of it, 'Morton's Fork' is the shabbiest piece of revenue-raising in history. But it wasn't only his greed for money. Everything about him is shabby, isn't it?"

"Yes. Dr. Gairdner wouldn't have any trouble in making *his* actions fit his character. How did you get on with the Doctor?"

"A fascinating study. But for the grace of God I think

151

the worthy Doctor might have made a living as a criminal."

"Because he cheated?"

"Because he didn't cheat. He was as honest as the day. He just couldn't reason from B to C."

"All right, I'll buy."

"Everyone can reason from A to B—even a child. And most adults can reason from B to C. But a lot can't. Most criminals can't. You may not believe it—I know it's an awful come-down from the popular conception of the criminal as a dashing and cute character—but the criminal mind is an essentially silly one. You can't imagine how silly sometimes. You'd have to experience it to believe their lack of reasoning powers. They arrive at B, but they're quite incapable of making the jump to C. They'll lay two completely incompatible things side by side and contemplate them with the most unquestioning content. You can't make them see that they can't have both, any more than you can make a man of no taste see that bits of plywood nailed on to a gable to simulate Tudor beams are impossible. Have you started your own book?"

"Well—I've made a sort of tentative beginning. I know the way I *want* to write it. I mean the form. I hope you won't mind."

"Why should I mind?"

"I want to write it the way it happened. You know; about my coming to see you, and our starting the Richard thing quite casually and not knowing what we were getting into, and how we stuck to things that actually happened and not what someone reported afterwards about it, and how we looked for the break in the normal pattern that would indicate where the mischief was, like bubbles coming up from a diver way below, and that sort of thing."

"I think it's a grand idea."

"You do?"

"I do indeed."

"Well, that's fine, then. I'll get on with it. I'm going to do some research on Henry, just as garnish. I'd like to be able to put their actual records side by side, you see. So that people can compare them for themselves. Did you know that Henry invented the Star Chamber?"

"Was it Henry? I'd forgotten that. Morton's Fork and
152

the Star Chamber. The classic sample of sharp practice, and the classic sample of tyranny. You're not going to have any difficulty in differentiating the rival portraits, are you? Morton's Fork and the Star Chamber make a nice contrast to the granting of the right to bail, and the prevention of the intimidation of juries."

"Was that Richard's Parliament? Golly, what a lot of reading I have to do. Atlanta's not speaking to me. She hates your marrow. She says I'm about as much use to a girl as last year's *Vogue*. But honestly, Mr. Grant, this is the first time in my life that anything exciting has happened to me. Important, I mean. Not exciting meaning exciting. Atlanta's exciting. She's all the excitement I ever want. But neither of us is important, the way I mean important—if you can understand what I mean."

"Yes, I understand. You've found something worth doing."

"That's it. I've found something worth doing. And it's me that's doing it; that's what's wonderful about it. Me. Mrs. Carradine's little boy. I come over here with Atlanta, with no idea about anything but using that research gag as an alibi. I walked into the B.M. to get me some dope to keep Pop quiet, and I walk out with a mission. Doesn't that shake you!" He eyed Grant in a considerng way. "You're quite sure, Mr. Grant, that you don't want to write this book yourself? After all, it's quite a thing to do."

"I shall *never* write a book," Grant said firmly. "Not even *My Twenty Years at the Yard*."

"What! Not even your autobiography?"

"Not even my autobiography. It is my considered opinion that far too many books are written as it is."

"But this is one that must be written," Carradine said, looking slightly hurt.

"Of course it is. This one must be written. Tell me: there's something I forgot to ask you. How soon after that double pardon did Tyrrel get that appointment in France? How soon after his supposed service to Henry in July 1486 did he become Constable of the Castle of Guisnes?"

Carradine stopped looking hurt and looked as malicious as it was possible for his kind woolly-lamb face to look.

"I was wondering when you were going to ask that," he
153

said. "I was going to throw it at you on my way out if you forgot to ask. The answer is: almost right away."

"So. Another appropriate little pebble in the mosaic. I wonder whether the constableship just happened to be vacant, or whether it was a French appointment because Henry wanted him out of England."

"I bet it was the other way about, and it was Tyrrel who wanted to get out of England. If I were being ruled by Henry VII, I'd sure prefer to be ruled by remote control. Especially if I had done a secret job for Henry that might make it convenient for Henry if I didn't live to too venerable an age."

"Yes, perhaps you're right. He didn't only go abroad, he stayed abroad—as we have already observed. Interesting."

"He wasn't the only one who stayed abroad. John Dighton did too. I couldn't find out who all the people who were supposed to be involved in the murder actually were. All the Tudor accounts are different, I suppose you know. Indeed most of them are so different that they contradict each other flat. Henry's pet historian, Polydore Virgil, says the deed was done when Richard was at York. According to the sainted More it was during an earlier trip altogether, when Richard was at Warwick. And the personnel changes with each account. So that it's difficult to sort them out. I don't know who Will Slater was—Black Will to you, and another piece of onomatopoesis—or Miles Forest. But there *was* a John Dighton. Grafton says he lived for long at Calais 'no less disdained than pointed at' and died there in great misery. How they relished a good moral, didn't they? The Victorians had nothing on them."

"If Dighton was destitute it doesn't look as if he had done any job for Henry. What was he by trade?"

"Well, if it's the same John Dighton, he was a priest, and he was anything but destitute. He was living very comfortably on the proceeds of a sinecure. Henry gave a John Dighton the living of Fulbeck, near Grantham—that's in Lincolnshire—on the 2nd of May, 1487."

"Well, well," Grant said, drawling. "1487. And he, too, lives abroad and in comfort."

"Uh-huh. Lovely, isn't it?"

"It's beautiful. And does anyone explain how the much-pointed-at Dighton wasn't haled home by the scruff of his neck to hang for regicide?"

"Oh, no. Nothing like that. Tudor historians didn't any of them think from B to C."

Grant laughed. "I see you're being educated."

"Sure. I'm not only learning history. I'm sitting at the feet of Scotland Yard on the subject of the human mind. Well, that will be about all for now. If you feel strong enough I'll read you the first two chapters of the book next time I come." He paused and said: "Would you mind, Mr. Grant, if I dedicated it to you?"

"I think you had better dedicate it to Carradine the Third," Grant said lightly.

But Carradine apparently did not feel it to be a light matter.

"I don't use soft soap as a dedication," he said, with a hint of stiffness.

"Oh, not soft soap," Grant said in haste. "A matter of policy merely."

"I'd never have started on this thing if it hadn't been for you, Mr. Grant," Carradine said, standing in the middle of the floor all formal and emotional and American and surrounded by the sweeping folds of his topcoat, "and I should like to make due acknowledgement of my indebtedness."

"I should be delighted, of course," murmured Grant, and the royal figure in the middle of the floor relaxed to boyhood again and the awkward moment was over. Carradine went away joyous and light-footed as he had come, looking thirty pounds heavier and twelve inches more round the chest than he had done three weeks ago.

And Grant took out the new knowledge that had been given him, hung it on the opposite wall, and stared at it.

CHAPTER SIXTEEN

She had been shut away from the world; that indestructibly virtuous beauty with the gilt hair.

Why gilt, he wondered for the first time. Silver-gilt probably; she had been radiantly fair. A pity that the word blonde had degenerated to the point where it had almost a secondary meaning.

She had been walled up to end her days where she could be no trouble to anyone. An eddy of trouble had moved with her all through her life. Her marriage to Edward had rocked England. She had been the passive means of Warwick's ruin. Her kindnesses to her family had built a whole new party in England and had prevented Richard's peaceful succession. Bosworth was implicit in that scanty little ceremony in the wilds of Northamptonshire when she became Edward's wife. But no one seemed to have borne her malice. Even the sinned-against Richard had forgiven her her relations' enormities. No one—until Henry came.

She had disappeared into obscurity. Elizabeth Woodville. The Queen Dowager who was mother of the Queen of England. The mother of the Princes in the Tower; who had lived free and prosperous under Richard III.

That was an ugly break in the pattern, wasn't it?

He took his mind away from personal histories and began to think police-fashion. It was time he tidied up his case. Put it shipshape for presenting. It would help the boy with his book, and better still it would clear his own mind. It would be down in black and white where he could see it.

He reached for his writing-pad and pen, and made a neat entry:

CASE: Disappearance of two boys (Edward, Prince of Wales; Richard, Duke of York) from the Tower of London, 1485 or thereabouts.

He wondered whether it would be better to do the two suspects in parallel columns or successively. Perhaps it was better to finish with Richard first. So he made another neat headline; and began on his summing-up:

RICHARD III

Previous Record:
Good. Has excellent record in public service, and good reputation in private life. Salient characteristic as indicated by his actions: good sense.

In the matter of the presumed crime:
(a) He did not stand to benefit; there were nine other heirs to the house of York, including three males.
(b) There is no contemporary accusation.
(c) The boys' mother continued on friendly terms with him until his death, and her daughters attended Palace festivities.
(d) He showed no fear of the other heirs of York, providing generously for their upkeep and granting all of them their royal state.
(e) His own right to the crown was unassailable, approved by Act of Parliament and public acclamation; the boys were out of the succession and of no danger to him.
(f) If he had been nervous about disaffection then the person to have got rid of was not the two boys, but the person who really was next in succession to him: young Warwick. Whom he publicly created his heir when his own son died.

Previous Record:

An adventurer, living at foreign courts. Son of an ambitious mother. Nothing known against his private life. No public office or employment. Salient characteristic as indicated by his actions: subtlety.

In the matter of the presumed crime:

(*a*) It was of great importance to him that the boys should not continue to live. By repealing the Act acknowledging the children's illegitimacy, he made the elder boy King of England, and the youngest boy the next heir.

(*b*) In the Act which he brought before Parliament for the attainting of Richard he accused Richard of the conventional tyranny and cruelty but made no mention of the two young Princes. The conclusion is inevitable that at that time the two boys were alive and their whereabouts known.

(*c*) The boys' mother was deprived of her living and consigned to a nunnery eighteen months after his succession.

(*d*) He took immediate steps to secure the persons of all the other heirs to the crown, and kept them in close arrest until he could with the minimum of scandal get rid of them.

(*e*) He had no right whatever to the throne. Since the death of Richard, young Warwick was *de jure* King of England.

It occurred to Grant for the first time, as he wrote it out, that it had been within Richard's power to legitimise his bastard son John, and foist him on the nation. There was no lack of precedent for such a course. After all, the whole Beaufort clan (including Henry's mother) were the descendants not only of an illegitimate union but of a double adultery. There was nothing to hinder Richard from legitimising that "active and well-disposed" boy who lived in recognised state in his household. It was surely the measure of Richard that no such course had apparently crossed his mind. He had appointed as his heir his brother's boy. Even in the destitution of his own grief, good sense was his ruling characteristic. Good sense and family feeling. No base-born son, however active and well-disposed, was going to sit in the Plantagenets' seat while his brother's son was there to occupy it.

It was remarkable how that atmosphere of family feeling permeated the whole story. All the way from Cicely's journeyings about in her husband's company to her son's free acknowledgement of his brother George's boy as his heir.

And it occurred to him too for the first time in full force just how that family atmosphere strengthened the case for Richard's innocence. The boys whom he was supposed to have put down as he would put down twin foals were Edward's sons; children he must have known personally and well. To Henry, on the other hand, they were mere symbols. Obstacles on a path. He may never even have set eyes on them. All questions of character apart, the choice between the two men as suspects might almost be decided on that alone.

It was wonderfully clearing to the head to see it neat and tidy as (a), (b), and (c). He had not noticed before how doubly suspect was Henry's behaviour over Titulus Regius. If, as Henry had insisted, Richard's claim was absurd, then surely the obvious thing to do was to have the thing reread in public and demonstrate its falsity. But he did no such thing. He went to endless pains to obliterate even the memory of it. The conclusion was inevitable that Richard's title to the crown as shown in Titulus Regius was unassailable.

CHAPTER SEVENTEEN

On the afternoon when Carradine reappeared in the room at the hospital Grant had walked to the window and back again, and was so cock-a-hoop about it that The Midget was moved to remind him that it was a thing that a child of eighteen months could do. But nothing could subdue Grant today.

"Thought you'd have me here for months, didn't you?" he crowed.

"We are very glad to see you better so quickly," she said primly; and added: "We are, of course, very glad, too, to have your bed."

And she clicked away down the corridor, all blond curls and starch.

Grant lay on his bed and looked at his little prison room with something approaching benevolence. Neither a man who has stood at the Pole nor a man who has stood on Everest has anything on a man who has stood at a window after weeks of being merely twelve stones of destitution. Or so Grant felt.

Tomorrow he was going home. Going home to be cosseted by Mrs. Tinker. He would have to spend half of each day in bed and he would be able to walk only with the aid of sticks, but he would be his own man again. At the bidding of no one. In tutelage to no half-pint piece of efficiency, yearned over by no lump of outsized benevolence.

It was a glorious prospect.

He had already unloaded his hallelujahs all over

Sergeant Williams, who had looked in on the completion of his chore in Essex, and he was now yearning for Marta to drop in so that he could peacock in front of her in his new-found manhood.

"How did you get on with the history books?" Williams had asked.

"Couldn't be better. I've proved them all wrong."

Williams had grinned. "I expect there's a law against that," he said. "MI 5 won't like it. Treason or lèse-majesté or something like that it might turn out to be. You never know nowadays. I'd be careful if I was you."

"I'll never again believe anything I read in a history book, as long as I live, so help me."

"You'll have to make exceptions," Williams pointed out with Williams' dogged reasonableness. "Queen Victoria was true, and I suppose Julius Caesar did invade Britain. And there's 1066."

"I'm beginning to have the gravest doubts about 1066. I see you've tied up the Essex job. What is Chummy like?"

"A thorough little bastard. Been treated soft all his life since he started stealing change from his Ma at the age of nine. A good belting at the age of twelve might have saved his life. Now he'll hang before the almond blossom's out. It's going to be an early spring. I've been working every evening in the garden this last few days, now that the days are drawing out. You'll be glad to sniff fresh air again."

And he had gone away, rosy and sane and balanced, as befitted a man who was belted for his good in his youth.

So Grant was longing for some other visitor from the outside world that he was so soon to be a part of again, and he was delighted when the familiar tentative tap came on his door.

"Come in, Brent!" he called, joyfully.

And Brent came in.

But it was not the Brent who had last gone out.

Gone was the jubilation. Gone was his newly acquired breadth.

He was no longer Carradine the pioneer, the blazer of trail.

He was just a thin boy in a very long, very large overcoat. He looked young, and shocked, and bereaved.

Grant watched him in dismay as he crossed the room with his listless unco-ordinated walk. There was no bundle of paper sticking out of his mail-sack of a pocket today.

Oh, well, thought Grant philosophically; it had been fun while it lasted. There was bound to be a snag somewhere. One couldn't do serious research in that light-hearted amateur way and hope to prove anything by it. One wouldn't expect an amateur to walk into the Yard and solve a case that had defeated the pro's; so why should he have thought himself smarter than the historians. He had wanted to prove to himself that he was right in his face-reading of the portrait; he had wanted to blot out the shame of having put a criminal on the bench instead of in the dock. But he would have to accept his mistake, and like it. Perhaps he had asked for it. Perhaps, in his heart of hearts, he had been growing a little pleased with himself about his eye for faces.

"Hullo, Mr. Grant."

"Hullo, Brent."

Actually it was worse for the boy. He was at the age when he expected miracles to happen. He was still at the age when he was surprised that a balloon should burst.

"You look saddish," he said cheerfully to the boy. "Something come unstuck?"

"Everything."

Carradine sat down on the chair and stared at the window.

"Don't these damned sparrows get you down?" he asked, fretfully.

"What is it? Have you discovered that there was a general rumour about the boys before Richard's death, after all?"

"Oh, much worse than that."

"Oh. Something in print? A letter?"

"No, it isn't that sort of thing at all. It's something much worse. Something quite—quite fundamental. I don't know how to tell you." He glowered at the quarrelling sparrows. "These damned birds. I'll never write that book now, Mr. Grant."

"Why not, Brent?"

"Because it isn't news to anyone. Everyone has known

162

all about those things all along."

"Known? About what?"

"About Richard not having killed the boys at all, and all that."

"They've *known?* Since when!"

"Oh, hundreds and hundreds of years."

"Pull yourself together, chum. It's only four hundred years altogether since the thing happened."

"I know. But it doesn't make any difference. People have known about Richard's not doing it for hundreds and hundreds—"

"Will you stop that keening and talk sense. When did this—this rehabilitation first begin?"

"Begin? Oh, at the first available moment."

"When was that?"

"As soon as the Tudors were gone and it was safe to talk."

"In Stuart times, you mean?"

"Yes, I suppose—yes. A man Buck wrote a vindication in the seventeenth century. And Horace Walpole in the eighteenth. And someone called Markham in the nineteenth."

"And who in the twentieth?"

"No one that I know of."

"Then what's wrong with your doing it?"

"But it won't be the same, don't you see? It won't be a great discovery!" He said it in capitals. A Great Discovery.

Grant smiled at him. "Oh, come! You can't expect to pick Great Discoveries off bushes. If you can't be a pioneer what's wrong with leading a crusade?"

"A crusade?"

"Certainly."

"Against what?"

"Tonypandy."

The boy's face lost its blankness. It looked suddenly amused, like someone who has just seen a joke.

"It's the damnedest silliest name, isn't it!" he remarked.

"If people have been pointing out for three hundred and fifty years that Richard didn't murder his nephews and a schoolbook can still say, in words of one syllable and without qualification, that he did, then it seems to me that Tonypandy has a long lead on you. It's time you got busy."

"But what can *I* do when people like Walpole and those have failed?"

"There's that old saying about constant water and its effect on stone."

"Mr. Grant, right now I feel an awfully feeble little trickle."

"You look it, I must say. I've never seen such self-pity. That's no mood to start bucking the British public in. You'll be giving enough weight away as it is."

"Because I've not written a book before, you mean?"

"No, that doesn't matter at all. Most people's first books are their best anyway; it's the one they wanted most to write. No, I meant that all the people who've never read a history book since they left school will feel themselves qualified to pontificate about what you've written. They'll accuse you of whitewashing Richard: 'whitewashing' has a derogatory sound that 'rehabilitation' hasn't, so they'll call it whitewashing. A few will look up the *Britannica*, and feel themselves competent to go a little further in the matter. These will slay you instead of flaying you. And the serious historians won't even bother to notice you."

"By God, I'll make them notice me!" Carradine said.

"Come! That sounds a little more like the spirit that won the Empire."

"We haven't got an Empire," Carradine reminded him.

"Oh, yes, you have," Grant said equably. "The only difference between ours and yours is that you acquire yours, economically, in the one latitude, while we got ours in bits all over the world. Had you written any of the book before the awful knowledge of its unoriginality hit you?"

"Yes, I'd done two chapters."

"What have you done with them? You haven't thrown them away, have you?"

"No. I nearly did. I nearly threw them in the fire."

"What stopped you?"

"It was an electric fire." Carradine stretched out his long legs in a relaxing movement and began to laugh. "Brother, I feel better already. I can't wait to land the

164

British public one in the kisser with a few home truths. Carradine the First is just raging in my blood."

"A very virulent fever, it sounds."

"He was the most ruthless old blackguard that ever felled timber. He started as a logger and ended up with a Renaissance castle, two yachts, and a private car. Railroad car, you know. It had green silk curtains with bobbles on them and inlay woodwork that had to be seen to be believed. It has been popularly supposed, not least by Carradine the Third, that the Carradine blood was growing thin. But right now I'm all Carradine the First. I know just how the old boy felt when he wanted to buy a particular forest and someone said that he couldn't have it. Brother, I'm going to town."

"That's nice," Grant said, mildly. "I was looking forward to that dedication." He took his writing-pad from the table and held it out. "I've been doing a policeman's summing-up. Perhaps it may help you when you come to your peroration."

Carradine took it and looked at it with respect.

"Tear it off and take it with you. I've finished with it."

"I suppose in a week or two you'll be too busy with real investigations to care about a—an academic one," Carradine said, a little wistfully.

"I'll never enjoy one more than I've enjoyed this," Grant said, with truth. He glanced sideways at the portrait which was still propped against the books. "I was more dashed than you would believe when you came in all despondent, and I thought it had come to pieces." He looked back at the portrait and said: "Marta thinks he is a little like Lorenzo the Magnificent. Her friend James thinks it is the face of a saint. My surgeon thinks it is the face of a cripple. Sergeant Williams thinks he looks like a great judge. But I think, perhaps, Matron comes nearest the heart of the matter."

"What does she say?"

"She says it is a face full of the most dreadful suffering."

"Yes. Yes, I suppose it is. And would you wonder, after all?"

"No. No, there was little he was spared. Those last two

years of his life must have happened with the suddenness and weight of an avalanche. Everything had been going along so nicely. England on an even keel at last. The civil war fading out of mind, a good firm government to keep things peaceful and a good brisk trade to keep things prosperous. It must have seemed a good outlook, looking out from Middleham across Wensleydale. And in two short years—his wife, his son, and his peace."

"I know one thing he was spared."

"What?"

"The knowledge that his name was to be a hissing and a byword down the centuries."

"Yes. That would have been the final heart-break. Do you know what I personally find *the* convincing thing in the case for Richard's innocence of any design for usurpation?"

"No. What?"

"The fact that he had to send for those troops from the North when Stillington broke his news. If he had had any fore-knowledge of what Stillington was going to say, or even any plans to concoct a story with Stillington's help, he would have brought those troops with him. If not to London then to the Home Counties where they would be handy. That he had to send urgently first to York and then to his Nevill cousins for men is proof that Stillington's confession took him entirely unawares."

"Yes. He came up with his train of gentlemen, expecting to take over the Regency. He met the news of the Woodville trouble when he came to Northampton, but that didn't rattle him. He mopped up the Woodville two thousand and went on to London as if nothing had happened. There was still nothing but an orthodox Coronation in front of him as far as he knew. It wasn't until Stillington confessed to the council that he sends for troops of his own. And he has to send all the way to the North of England at a critical moment. Yes, you're right, of course. He was taken aback." He propped the leg of his spectacles with a forefinger in the old tentative gesture, and proffered a companion piece. "Know what I find the convincing thing in the case for Henry's guilt?"

"What?"

166

"The mystery."

"Mystery?"

"The mysteriousness. The hush-hush. The hole-and-corner stuff."

"Because it is in character, you mean?"

"No, no; nothing as subtle as that. Don't you see: Richard had no need of any mystery; but Henry's whole case depended on the boys' end being mysterious. No one has ever been able to think up a reason for such a hole-and-corner method as Richard was supposed to have used. It was a quite mad way to do it. He couldn't hope to get away with it. Sooner or later he was going to have to account for the boys not being there. As far as he knew he had a long reign in front of him. No one has ever been able to think why he should have chosen so difficult and dangerous a way when he had so many simpler methods at hand. He had only to have the boys suffocated, and let them lie in state while the whole of London walked by and wept over two young things dead before their time of fever. That is the way he *would* have done it, too. Goodness, *the whole point* of Richard's killing the boys was to prevent any rising in their favour, and to get any benefit from the murder the fact of their deaths would *have* to be made public, and as soon as possible. It would defeat the whole plan if people didn't *know* that they were dead. But Henry, now. Henry *had* to find a way to push them out of sight. Henry *had* to be mysterious. Henry *had* to hide the facts of when and how they died. *Henry's whole case* depended on no one's knowing what exactly happened to the boys."

"It did indeed, Brent; it did indeed," Grant said, smiling at counsel's eager young face. "You ought to be at the Yard, Mr. Carradine!"

Brent laughed.

"I'll stick to Tonypandy," he said. "I bet there's a lot more of it that we don't know about. I bet history books are just riddled with it."

"You'd better take Sir Cuthbert Oliphant with you, by the way." Grant took the fat respectable-looking volume from his locker. "Historians should be compelled to take a course in psychology before they are allowed to write."

"Huh. That wouldn't do anything for them. A man who is interested in what makes people tick doesn't write history. He writes novels, or becomes an alienist, or a magistrate—"

"Or a confidence man."

"Or a confidence man. Or a fortune-teller. A man who understands about people hasn't any yen to write history. History is toy soldiers."

"Oh, come. Aren't you being a little severe? It's a very learned and erudite—"

"Oh, I didn't mean it that way. I mean: it's moving little figures about on a flat surface. It's half-way to mathematics, when you come to think about it."

"Then if it's mathematics they've no right to drag in backstairs gossip," Grant said, suddenly vicious. The memory of the sainted More continued to upset him. He thumbed through the fat respectable Sir Cuthbert in a farewell review. As he came to the final pages the progress of the paper from under his thumb slackened, and presently stopped.

"Odd," he said, "how willing they are to grant a man the quality of courage in battle. They have only tradition to go on, and yet not one of them questions it. Not one of them, in fact, fails to stress it."

"It was an enemy's tribute," Carradine reminded him. "The tradition began with a ballad written by the other side."

"Yes. By a man of the Stanleys. 'Then a knight to King Richard gan say.' It's here somewhere." He turned over a leaf or two, until he found what he was looking for. "It was 'good Sir William Harrington,' it seems. The knight in question.

"There may no man their strokes abide, the Stanleys dints they be so strong [the treacherous bastards!]
Ye may come back at another tide, methinks ye tarry here too long,
Your horse at your hand is ready, another day you may worship win
And come to reign with royalty, and wear your crown and be our king.

'Nay, give me my battle-axe in my hand, set the crown of England on my head so high.

For by Him that made both sea and land, King of England this day I will die.

One foot I will never flee whilst the breath is my breast within.'

As he said so did it be—if he lost his life he died a King."

" 'Set the crown of England on my head,' " said Carradine, musing. "That was the crown that was found in a hawthorn bush afterwards."

"Yes. Set aside for plunder probably."

"I used to picture it one of those high plush things that King George got crowned in, but it seems it was just a gold circlet."

"Yes. It could be worn outside the battle helmet."

"Gosh," said Carradine with sudden feeling, "I sure would have hated to wear that crown if I had been Henry! I sure would have hated it!" He was silent for a little, and then he said: "Do you know what the town of York wrote—wrote in their records, you know—about the battle of Bosworth?"

"No."

"They wrote: 'This day was our good King Richard piteously slain and murdered; to the great heaviness of this city.' "

The chatter of the sparrows was loud in the quiet.

"Hardly the obituary of a hated usurper," Grant said at last, very dry.

"No," said Carradine. "No. 'To the great heaviness of this city,' " he repeated slowly, rolling the phrase over in his mind. "They cared so much about it that even with a new régime in the offing and the future not to be guessed at they put down in black and white in the town record their opinion that it was murder and their sorrow at it."

"Perhaps they had just heard about the indignities perpetrated on the King's dead body and were feeling a little sick."

"Yes. Yes. You don't like to think of a man you've

known and admired flung stripped and dangling across a pony like a dead animal."

"One wouldn't like to think of even an enemy so. But sensibility is not a quality that one would look for among the Henry-Morton crowd."

"Huh. Morton!" said Brent, spitting out the word as if it were a bad taste. "No one was 'heavy' when Morton died, believe me. Know what the Chronicler wrote of him? The London one, I mean. He wrote: 'In our time was no man like to be compared with him in all things; albeit that he lived not without the great disdain and hatred of the Commons of this land.' "

Grant turned to look at the portrait which had kept him company through so many days and nights.

"You know," he said, "for all his success and his Cardinal's hat I think Morton was the loser in that fight with Richard III. In spite of his defeat and his long traducing, Richard came off the better of these two. He was loved in his day."

"That's no bad epitaph," the boy said soberly.

"No. Not at all a bad epitaph," Grant said, shutting Oliphant for the last time. "Not many men would ask for a better." He handed over the book to its owner. "Few men have earned so much," he said.

When Carradine had gone Grant began to sort out the things on his table, preparatory to his homegoing on the morrow. The unread fashionable novels could go to the hospital library to gladden other hearts than his. But he would keep the book with the mountain pictures. And he must remember to give The Amazon back her two history books. He looked them out so that he could give them to her when she brought in his supper. And he read again, for the first time since he began his search for the truth about Richard, the schoolbook tale of his villainy. There it was, in unequivocable black and white, the infamous story. Without a perhaps or a peradventure. Without a qualification or a question.

As he was about to shut the senior of the two educators his eye fell on the beginning of Henry VII's reign, and he read: "It was the settled and considered policy of the Tudors to rid themselves of all rivals to the throne, more

170

especially those heirs of York who remained alive on the succession of Henry VII. In this they were successful, although it was left to Henry VIII to get rid of the last of them."

He stared at this bald announcement. This placid acceptance of wholesale murder. This simple acknowledgement of a process of family elimination.

Richard III had been credited with the elimination of two nephews, and his name was a synonym for evil. But Henry VII, whose "settled and considered policy" was to eliminate a whole family was regarded as a shrewd and far-seeing monarch. Not very lovable perhaps, but constructive and painstaking, and very successful withal.

Grant gave up. History was something that he would never understand.

The values of historians differed so radically from any values with which he was acquainted that he could never hope to meet them on any common ground. He would go back to the Yard, where murderers were murderers and what went for Cox went equally for Box.

He put the two books tidily together and when The Amazon came in with his mince and stewed prunes he handed them over with a neat little speech of gratitude. He really was very grateful to The Amazon. If she had not kept her school books he might never have started on the road that led to his knowledge of Richard Plantagenet.

She looked confused by his kindness, and he wondered if he had been such a bear in his illness that she expected nothing but carping from him. It was a humiliating thought.

"We'll miss you, you know," she said, and her big eyes looked as if they might brim with tears. "We've grown used to having you here. We've even got used to *that*." And she moved an elbow in the direction of the portrait.

A thought stirred in him.

"Will you do something for me?" he asked.

"Of course. Anything I can do."

"Will you take that photograph to the window and look at it in a good light as long as it takes to count a pulse?"

"Yes, of course, if you want me to. But why?"

171

"Never mind why. You just do it to please me. I'll time you."

She took up the portrait and moved into the light of the window.

He watched the second-hand of his watch.

He gave her forty-five seconds and then said: "Well?" And as there was no immediate answer he said again: "Well?"

"Funny," she said. "When you look at it for a little it's really quite a nice face, isn't it?"

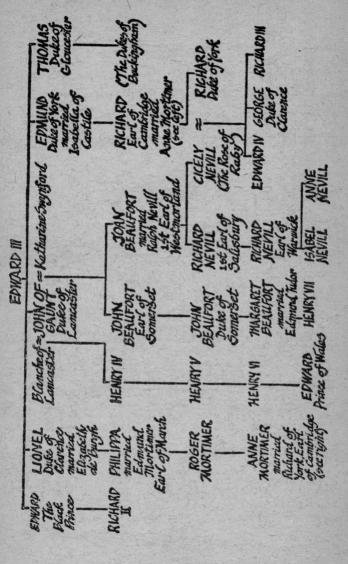

EDWARD III

EDWARD The Black Prince — LIONEL Duke of Clarence married Elizabeth de Burgh — Blanche of Lancaster = JOHN OF GAUNT Duke of Lancaster = Katharine Swynford — EDMUND Duke of York married Isabella of Castile — THOMAS Duke of Gloucester

RICHARD II — PHILLIPA married Edmund Mortimer Earl of March — HENRY IV — JOHN BEAUFORT Earl of Somerset — JOAN BEAUFORT married Ralph Nevill 1st Earl of Westmorland — RICHARD Earl of Cambridge married Anne Mortimer (see left)

ROGER MORTIMER — HENRY V — JOHN BEAUFORT Duke of Somerset — RICHARD NEVILL 1st Earl of Salisbury — CICELY NEVILL (The Rose of Raby) = RICHARD Duke of York — RICHARD (The Duke of Buckingham)

ANNE MORTIMER married Richard of York, Earl of Cambridge (see right) — HENRY VI — MARGARET BEAUFORT married Edmund Tudor — RICHARD NEVILL Earl of Warwick — EDWARD IV — GEORGE Duke of Clarence — RICHARD III

EDWARD Prince of Wales — HENRY VII — ISABEL NEVILL — ANNE NEVILL

174

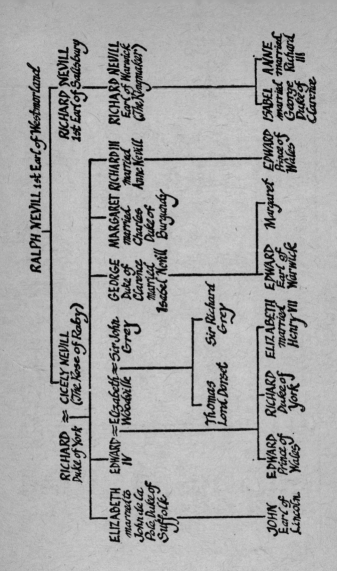